$\mathcal{V}$OICES OF THE $\mathcal{S}$OUTH

OTHER BOOKS BY SHIRLEY ANN GRAU

The Black Prince and Other Stories
The Hard Blue Sky
The Keepers of the House
The Condor Passes
The Wind Shifting West
Evidence of Love
Nine Women
Roadwalkers

THE HOUSE ON
COLISEUM
STREET

THE
HOUSE ON COLISEUM STREET

Shirley Ann Grau

LOUISIANA STATE UNIVERSITY PRESS
BATON ROUGE AND LONDON

Copyright © 1961, 1989 by Shirley Ann Grau
LSU Press edition published 1996 by arrangement with the author
First published by Alfred A. Knopf, Inc.
All rights reserved
Manufactured in the United States of America
05 04 03 02 01 00 99 98 97 96   5 4 3 2 1

Library of Congress Cataloging-in-Publication Data
Grau, Shirley Ann.
    The house on Coliseum Street / Shirley Ann Grau.
        p.   cm. — (Voices of the South)
    ISBN 0-8071-2101-0 (pbk. : alk. paper)
    1. Southern States—Fiction.   I. Title.   II. Series.
PS3557.R283H68   1996
813'.54—dc20   96-19612
                                                            CIP

The paper in this book meets the guidelines for permanence and durability of the
Committee on Production Guidelines for Book Longevity of the Council on Library
Resources.♾

THE HOUSE ON COLISEUM STREET

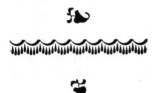

JOAN MITCHELL sat in the green painted gazebo that stood in the far corner of her great-aunt's lawn, the corner overlooking the Gulf. She had been there most of the afternoon, playing one game of solitaire after the other, shuffling the cards in fancy river-boat gambler fashion. Now she stopped her game to watch a rainstorm move up out of the Gulf. She had been aware of it for some time. Even without looking she had felt its approach, had felt a change, that was really little more than a quiver in the air.

She tossed the cards aside; some of them slid across the table and dropped to the floor. She glanced after them but didn't bother picking them up.

She turned and knelt on the padded bench that lined

the octagonal house and peered through an opening in the crisscross lattice that formed the walls. Beyond the gazebo, some thirty or forty feet of slow slope, was the low iron fence that edged the property. Beyond that the ground dropped sharply to the four-lane coast highway, the beach, and the Gulf.

She could see the rain, a grey haze like smoke, at Dolphin Island, some five miles off shore. She could smell it now too, the wonderful exciting smell of coming rain. The quiver in the air grew stronger.

The island disappeared in the haze. And the little tendrils of Virginia creeper that streaked the outside of the trellis began to shiver slightly. Joan got an extra pillow and shoved it behind her knees and settled down to watch.

In ten minutes the first drops came, big tadpole-shaped drops that plopped and exploded with sharp, distinct sounds. And then the rain itself—windless sheets, straight down, luminous grey, fish-colored. The roof began to leak. She counted the places, three, four, and some bubbles near the edge that would soon be a steady drain. She glanced over her shoulder and saw a little stream pour down on the cards. She saw a jack of diamonds jump and shiver.

There was the smell of settling dust now, and all the different noises of the rain—rattles and drips and hisses.

The small rain, she thought. And the poem she had read only last night came popping into her head:

O western wind, when wilt thou blow
That the small rain down can rain?
Christ, that my love were in my arms
And I in my bed again!

It was such a silly thing to think of. "Damn," she said
aloud. Reading too much. When there was nothing else
to do. Nothing but sit. When talking was too much
trouble. And your body was so light and hollow that you
wondered sometimes whether the wind would get inside
it, behind it, and blow it over and over. It was so light,
it was so dry. . . .

Joan held out her hand and looked at it, and she felt a
little tingle of surprise. It wasn't dry or withered, but it
felt that way. . . .

"Damn," she said aloud again. It wasn't making
sense. . . . Come back, old girl, she told herself, before
you get into orbit.

She looked at her body, carefully. It was round and
plump (I've been eating too much, she thought) and
tanned a dark brown.

Water was dripping on her head. She lifted one hand,
absent-mindedly. Then jumped. And giggled. And
moved aside, settling down finally in a dry spot.

The squall passed over slowly. On the other side the
sun was bright and hard and the sky was brilliant cloud-
less blue.

There was a burst of traffic on the highway below her.

The rain would have held them up, and now they'd be driving like crazy to catch even. And who would they be, she thought, the people in those cars—kids from the air base, most likely, she answered herself. Thin-faced kids in grey uniforms, heading for New Orleans on a week-end pass. And other people going into the city for something—a game maybe. There was always some sort of athletics on week ends.

Lots and lots of people moving along the highway. Her mother, Aurelie, would be on the road. Coming to take her back to New Orleans. Of course. She lived there. She had always lived there. In the house on Coliseum Street. She had been born there twenty years ago. Her great-great-grandfather built that house, way back a long time ago, she'd forgot just how long, but one year when the price of sugar was high.

It was her mother's house now. It was Aurelie Caillet's house. (She always thought of her mother as Aurelie Caillet, always by her maiden name.) And someday it would pass to her, Joan Mitchell. Because she was the oldest. . . .

She didn't want to go home. Maybe because she had the funniest feeling that the house wasn't real, wasn't there at all. Nor the people in it. . . . She felt different here on the coast. Not happy, perhaps. But sure. She hadn't been this sure since she was a child and had gone into the library (a small dark room, its air laced by the carbolic smell of bindings and the sweet odor of mildew, and in a little secretary, carefully locked against the children, the family-written books: one or two on law, three volumes of travel, some of devotion, one of poetry) and had puzzled over a big globe, turning it carefully around and around until she found the spot she wanted. She put her finger on it and said aloud: "I am here. Right here."

Years later, one evening—just last year—when she'd felt particularly confused, she'd remembered and gone back to the globe. And turned it and looked at it. But it wasn't the same. The names of the countries were different. All the possessions were different. And though she'd stood looking at it for a long time it didn't do any good.

She felt that way in the house on Coliseum Street. Maybe it was because her four half-sisters lived there too. Her mother had been married five times and had had a daughter by each husband. Joan had to stop sometimes and figure out just whose father was who. When she was little she'd even had trouble remembering her sisters' last names.

On the coast the air seemed lighter and clearer, especially when a wind blew from across the Gulf. Even now, in September.

She remembered New Orleans. The close windless heat of a river town. The swamp smell after the daily rain. The oleander bushes with their glossy thriving poisonous leaves. The grass and vines that grew so frantically you could see them move—the way you could see the heavy white moonflowers open on summer nights, the way they unfolded in the heat, stretching until their backs were broken and they flopped open and died. And the sky was like a teacup fitted overhead, close and hard and shiny as china.

But she lived there. In the house on Coliseum Street.

She was Joan Claire Mitchell, daughter of Aurelie Caillet and Anthony Mitchell. She had been baptized that way in the Cathedral, and she had been confirmed there. Her name was written on the back of the cross on her crystal rosary. Somewhere. She had put that away the morning she came back from the confirmation ceremony, wearing her white taffeta dress and long white stockings, and her veil like a bride's on her head. She had taken everything, including her specially made slip, all tucks and embroidery, folded them in a box and put the cover on. She did not look at them again. She had not even thought about them until today.

More cars swooped by on the road, weaving, tooting madly. In one of them, she thought, Aurelie will be coming over. To take me back.

I could have taken the train. Or maybe she didn't think I would take the train by myself. Maybe she thought the only way to get me back was to come get me. . . . But that isn't fair. It's mean, and it isn't fair at all. I must be sick or something. Thinking like that.

She's been real great. For sure. All through the mess. There wouldn't be many mothers'd take it like that. Not a complaint.

Just a little finger tapping silence. And a trip to the

window to stare out, even though the outside blinds were closed tight and bolted against the hot afternoon sun.

Just a question. Only one: "How long has it been?" Two and a half, nearly three, months. Then another close inspection of the closed blinds.

"It will have to be done at once. I'll call Aunt Ethel. You can stop there. Over at the Pass."

She remembered every word. Even the way her mother said stop for stay.

And she remembered how relieved she'd been when she no longer had to figure things out alone. Her mother did not even bother asking her. She went ahead and arranged.

Not many others, Joan thought, would have taken it like that.

The cards on the table were soaking. Their edges were ruffling out with the water. She gathered them up and wiped them on her skirt. She pressed them together between her fingers, trying to get the layers of paper to stick together.

She sat very still, listening as she had come to do over these past weeks. Listening to the caverns of emptiness inside her. Listening to her heart beat out, echoing in the arches of bone and flesh. The empty arches.

She felt so light. Her feet just brushed the ground. She reached out one hand and held fast to the doorjamb so she shouldn't float away up and out of reach. She stood and watched her fingers holding on. Until a little brown lizard ran up the frame and crossed over her knuckles. And she felt his hard scurrying little feet.

She heard the sound she had been waiting for, the sound that stood out above the noisy dripping of the leaves, and the steady sucking of the sandy ground, and the fluttering of the birds. The sound of tires on the graveled drive.

They had come. It was time to go back.

She took the cushions and piled them all together on one corner of the bench. She would have to bring them in. The dew would leave them blotched with black mold by morning.

A couple of blue jays came to peck at the lawn, their feathers brilliant and glossy as they stabbed about in the blades of grass. And her aunt's old woman's voice called over the dripping garden: "Joan! Company for you!"

"I'll be right there."

She gathered the cushions in her arms and started back.

There were so many, they were piled so high, that she could not see the ground over them. Somehow she got off the brick path and was walking over the soaking soggy grass. She shrugged and kept on walking. She even remembered a little tune to hum under her breath as she went.

She saw Aurelie first. But then you always saw Aurelie first—saw her tall thin figure and great head, heavy head, with masses of reddish brown hair pulled straight back into an old-fashioned roll, and a face with clear high cheekbones like an Indian, a hooked Creole nose, and large dark brown eyes streaked with bright yellow.

Aurelie was hugging her: "Child, you're brown as a berry!" And over her shoulder Joan's eyes were looking for the other figure she had known would be there. She found him finally: Fred Aleman. He kissed her politely on the cheek. She caught a quick smell of starch and shaving lotion. His shoulder felt good to her hand— solid, strong. He was more handsome than she had remembered—tall, heavy, with olive skin and straight black hair.

"Fred," she said, "I'm so glad you came."

"My pleasure, ma'am." He was mocking her gently, smiling, and she felt the way she always did with him— familiar, comfortable as if she had always known him.

Standing there with the two of them, she found it hard to believe that she had ever been away.

LATE that evening they drove up to the house on Coliseum Street.

Like all the others on that street the house was narrow and three stories tall, white painted and black shuttered. The first two floors had porches straight across the front, narrow porches edged and ornamented with light lacy ironwork. A slender delicate house of the sort that had been popular in the 1840's. In front was a tiny lawn divided exactly in two by a brick walk and edged by the scrolls and feathers of a low iron fence. In one of those smooth tiny patches of grass, misplaced and hideous, was a fountain, a bubbling fountain.

Its tile basin was mottled with garish blue and yellow mosaics of fish and shells. In its center stood a young mermaid, a pitcher spilling water over her shoulder. From the sides of the circle four bronze dolphins spat short streams of water at her feet.

Her father's fountain. . . . Anthony Mitchell had built it during the year he had lived in the house, the single year of his marriage to Aurelie. He had designed it himself and watched over its construction carefully. He had protected it in his divorce settlement. He had protected it even more securely in his will. The fountain would stay. Aurelie's regular—and very large—monthly check depended on it.

"The neighborhood looks the same," Joan said.

"Did you expect a change?" Aurelie asked.

"I guess not." Joan asked: "Are the kids home?"

"My dear," Aurelie said, "you really have lost track of time. Only Doris. The others are at camp."

"Oh," Joan said. "Of course. How silly of me."

She scarcely saw her three youngest sisters. They were away at school, they were away at camp. She saw them only on holidays. When they were all children, when the youngest was no more than three, they had a song to sing on those days. A song made up of their names that they sang to a kind of Elizabethan round Aurelie had taught them: Joan, Doris, Phyllis, Celine, Ann. Aurelie's friends were tremendously impressed.

It sounded really very nice. . . .

"The same house," Aurelie was saying, "and the same people in it!"

The tiny fountain winked at Joan as they went up the front walk. The brilliant yellow tiles gleamed even in the half light of the evening.

Fred took her suitcase into the hall and put it at the foot of the stairs. Joan put her train case beside it. She asked: "Don't you think we could have a drink?"

Aurelie's eyebrows went up in mock horror. "And

you, my dear?" she said to Fred. "Will you join us?" As she spoke, she had already slipped an arm through his and was leading him into the living room. Joan followed.

The living room was on the east side—the shady side —of the house, but even so the blinds were kept shut. It was always quite dark and there was very little air moving. But it was cool. A damp cool coming from the large tubs of fern that were fitted carefully into the corners off the edges of the rug.

"A gin and tonic would be nice, don't you think?" Aurelie opened the old-fashioned secretary that had been turned into a bar. She mixed the drinks swiftly with all the assurance of a professional bartender. She fixed a plain tonic for herself; she did not drink. Alcohol, she said, made lines in women's faces much too early. She preferred to miss the exhilaration and save her face.

She wrapped the glasses, which had immediately started to drip in the damp heavy air, in little embroidered napkins. "You know," she said, "great-uncle Henry would just die if he could see what we have done with his secretary. He was a teetotaler, you know."

"That's right," Fred said. "He was, wasn't he?"

He knows that as well as I do, Joan thought with a sudden rush of fierceness. He is only saying it because she would like him to. He's always doing what other people want him to do, to make them feel better.

Fred was sitting on the little rosewood sofa now, the

one that had just been reupholstered in a tapestry design of diamonds and flowers. He was saying politely: "I've never had the chance to look him up, not in any complete way. Not the way I want to. He was a remarkable man, and I know something about him, of course. A pioneer. A man of real vision."

Joan heard Aurelie's voice making some answer, but she closed her ears and talked angrily to herself. Horse shit, she told herself, he didn't do anything. Except get to be governor on bought votes during the Reconstruction. And live to be eighty. And make a little money on sugar cane. And survive a couple of depressions. And outlive all his children. And see his great-grandchildren get married.

Her mother's voice jarred her back. "Dear child," Aurelie was saying, "you are sitting there with a frightful frown on your pretty face. And you are talking to yourself in a most animated fashion."

The edge in the tone warned her. She certainly did not want to endure her mother's temper. "I am sorry," Joan said. "A car trip always leaves me a little groggy and far away."

"The drink would help," Fred said gently.

He's heard that note in her voice too, she thought. It's sweet of him to give me a way out.

He was talking to her mother again. I wonder, Joan thought, does she know that he doesn't hear a word she's saying, that he's watching me? That he's worrying about me, wondering if there's anything wrong?

And in spite of herself she felt a little shiver of excitement—the shiver that was a mixture of gratitude and attraction toward a man.

Why not? she asked herself silently. I'm not bad looking and I'm not old. I'm supposed to like it. He's a nice guy and handsome, except for his ears. Of course. And it's lovely to have somebody wondering about you.

She had been thinking more slowly than she realized. More time must have passed than she knew, because it was Fred who finally turned to her with a smile and said: "Come back, little Joan."

She jumped in her chair, as if somebody had touched her, and looked very guilty.

Aurelie chuckled. Lay back her large head and laughed aloud, a robust laugh that clashed sharply with her tinkling speech.

Joan blushed, feeling very silly. "I've been alone a lot this summer," she said, "and I suppose I got in the habit of talking to myself."

"We were just teasing," Fred said.

"My dear, you looked so silly," Aurelie said.

Then Joan was furious with herself for trying to explain. It's none of their business, she said fiercely and silently. And I don't have to explain anything at all. Not one thing.

She stood up and this time she said aloud: "I suppose I am tired. I really should lie down awhile."

She was at the door before she realized that Fred was talking to her. "What?"

"I thought we were going to dinner—or would you rather not?"

Why so patient? Why was he always so kind?

"Mother will go with you," Joan said, deliberately using a word Aurelie disliked. "I'm fine right here."

Fred shrugged. (How Cajun he looks when he does that, Joan thought.) "I had hoped . . ."

"Silly boy," Joan said, "Mother would love to go. And I promise not to be a bit jealous."

She turned up the stairs, grabbing the little train case as she went, hurrying so she would not be tempted to look at Aurelie's face.

HER room had not changed. The same mahogany furniture with the cracked dull finish, the result of years of careful oiling and long hot summers. The windows were closed, the whole bank of windows that faced east and dribbled light into her eyes every single morning of the world. Of her world.

Nice old room, she found herself thinking. But that wasn't possible. Ever since she was little she had wanted to get away. And the times she had actually been away—at camp or on a holiday—she had not missed it at all. Now, as she went about opening the windows and opening the screens and blowing the accumulation of gnats and moths out of the window sill, and shaking a faint film of dust off the organdy curtains, there was an ache in her chest that was an actual pain.

How funny, she thought. How very funny.

She turned back the covers on the bed and sniffed the musty odor of the sheets. No one had changed them. The room wasn't touched.

She slipped off her dress and loosened her bra and stretched out on the bed.

She listened to the last afternoon sounds, sounds she
had been hearing ever since she was an infant. The yell-
ing of children playing Devil on the Banquette in the
shade of the thick old camphor trees across the street.
. . . They said the trees were planted as a protection
against fever, that if you had a camphor tree outside
your house and wore some of the aromatic berries in a
little cloth bag around your neck along with a little voo-
doo skin bag, you didn't get yellow fever. But just in
case you did, you planted a sweet olive tree by the front
gate. So that people coming in for funerals could break
off a sprig of the waxy heavy sweet flowers—the tree
was always in bloom—and carry it into the parlor where
the corpse was. . . . It must have come in handy on
the long hot summer days, she thought. . . . The
sweet olive by the front gate of the house on Coliseum
Street was enormous, and it must have been very old because it grew so very slowly. Dead man's bush. Aurelie
hated it, but she didn't do anything about it.

I'd hire me a couple of Negroes with an ax and a saw,
Joan thought, and get it cut down. None of this waiting
around and putting off and sitting back and saying
you're going to do something. Me, I'd go right ahead
and get it done.

Even as she said that to herself, she didn't believe it.
The slow windless dusk was getting to her, seeping in
until the sharp decisive lines were gone, and nothing
was really too important.

She got up and took off her slip and bra and panties

and lay down naked and felt the soft warmth all around her, the air that was heavy and thick and soft as water. The children stopped playing and went home to rest before supper. An old-clothes man passed by with his wagon and clanking bell that shook out flat sounds into the evening.

I shouldn't have come back. I should have found a way to go off somewhere. But I didn't. I wonder why I didn't.

I'm back and caught just where I was four months ago. Where I said I wouldn't ever be again. I came back, I came back. Whatever happens, I did it.

Something else came out of the soft bright dusk, a lonesome twitching that wasn't so much physical as it was emotional.

And it's worse. Because I didn't love Michael then, but I love him now. And how did that happen? I didn't love him last June. Not even the day we went hunting for the stuffed owls. . . .

Last June. That was when it started. Way back. Four months ago. On a close hot morning last June.

I. JUNE

3

COLISEUM STREET was quiet. There was no traffic, there never was. The houses always looked closed and deserted, their galleries dusty and empty. No one ever walked by. The sidewalks—the banquettes, people on Coliseum Street still called them—had been cracked and broken by the roots of the oaks and camphors and magnolias that shaded the street and turned its surface into a slippery sludge when it rained. Only occasionally a wino or a mainliner would come stumbling along, straying from the slums a dozen blocks or so away, over by the levees that guarded the river. And then, routinely, one of the householders would telephone the police.

The police came quickly too, not because the people along the street had very much money (they didn't; the houses were slightly shabby and always a couple of seasons behind in their paint) but because they were persistent and noisy and had large families of cousins and aunts and uncles who were vaguely connected with the city government. And because generations past, the

23

owners of the houses had been rich. The memory of wealth is still a kind of power in New Orleans.

That particular morning, a Tuesday, the second of June, one of the strays entered the street. He stood for awhile at the corner, squinting into the leafy corridor. He moved down into it for half a block, stopping again to squint up at the trees, taking off his old felt hat and wiping his face with it.

The street closed up on itself, like a doodlebug rolling into a ball. The houseboy who had been hosing down the front walk at the Forstalls left his hose, pausing only to turn off the water, and disappeared around the back. The Edwards' maid, a tall skinny black woman who had spent most of the morning sweeping and cleaning the front porch so that she could see who was entertaining for lunch, flicked back into the door with only a switch of her yellow uniform. A nurse came and got the Villere girl who was playing in her swing in the side yard of the corner house. She yanked her out of the swing without a word and carried her off screaming and kicking.

All down the street the windows that looked out on the front porches (the windows that were nearly always kept open for a cross breeze) were closing. There was a little flutter all along Coliseum Street, as if a wind was blowing. But of course it wasn't. There was never a wind in the middle of a June morning.

The man had put his hat back on his head now, and he moved along. The uneven sidewalks with their sharp angles seemed to bother him. He stumbled and swayed once and steadied himself with a hand to the trunk of an oak tree. He went a bit farther, then fell over the broken pavement. He did not seem to try to get up.

He was then directly in front of the Caillet house. His outflung hand was a few inches away from the wrought-iron pillar that supported the iron gate.

Inside the house, people were watching. No one had told them to, no one had to. They had simply happened to look out.

Joan Mitchell stood in the upstairs front hall—she had opened one of the shutters—and watched. She squinted and craned her neck forward. It was very hard to see from this angle. Through the twisting crooked limbs of the camphor tree, the figure seemed putty colored, seemed to fade into the concrete walk.

The still sunny minutes passed. You could almost hear them clacking by like a metronome. Mockingbirds in the big oak began to screech and fight.

"For heaven's sake, child!"

Joan jumped and turned guiltily. Her mother had come up behind her.

"Close the window, you silly child!" Aurelie was wearing a robe of silky purple-flowered print. She never got dressed before ten. "Close the window, child," she repeated. "Don't be so silly."

"Not way up here."

"Honestly, there are times when I just don't know what to think of you."

"I'm twenty feet up," Joan said.

"Really, now . . ."

"I was listening. He was saying something."

"Don't listen to him."

"I think he's saying water. Or something like that."

Aurelie folded her arms. It was a gesture she used only when she was extremely angry. "My dear girl," she said, "if you would stop being such an obstinate silly little ass, you would not resemble your father so much."

Joan shrugged and went back to her watching.

"As a man," Aurelie said, "he was entitled to do silly things if he wished. Perhaps."

Her arm reached around Joan and closed the window.

"Behave like six, get treated like six." The arms folded. "I'll stay right here until the police come."

"What do you suppose they do with them?" Joan asked.

"How on earth should I know?"

"You hear about the way they handle them."

"Don't be such a silly child."

Joan pushed her nose against the shirred curtain that covered the glass and tried to see. But the glass in the window was old and wavy and the image was distorted beyond recognition. Still, with her mother there, she had to stay. They waited in silence, Joan breathing in the softly fragrant dust of the cloth. It seemed a very, very long time.

When the police had gone, and the windows all along Coliseum Street had opened up again, Joan went out the front door and looked down at the broken spot of banquette where the man had been. She almost expected to find something. A shadow left behind. But there was nothing. Only the greyish cement with its pebbly underside showing through the widest cracks.

She stood awhile, waiting. But nothing happened. The Villere girl twisted the swing up tightly, then sat and whirled with it, was dizzy, and vomited in the dusty azalea bed.

He called that same morning. Joan did not recognize his voice. "It's Michael Kern," he said.

"Oh," she said, "oh goodness yes." She had seen him only a half dozen times, the last when he had come to the house on Coliseum Street to date her sister Doris, who at eighteen was not quite two years younger.

"Will you go out with me tonight?" he asked abruptly.

"I'm not Doris," she said. "She's gone out somewhere."

"To hell with Doris," he said. "I'm asking you if you have a date tonight."

It was a Tuesday and Fred Aleman, her steady, always went to the Athletic Club to play handball on Tuesday nights. So he would not be coming by.

"Don't get angry," he said, "I just thought that when I met you at your house, I just thought you might want to go out with me."

It wasn't much of an invitation, Joan thought. It wasn't anything of an invitation.

She still hadn't said anything. "Well," he said finally, puzzled by the silence, "you can't shoot a man for trying. And if you weren't doing anything I thought it might be fun to go out to the lake for crabs and beer."

"The lake?"

"You didn't expect the Blue Room on my salary?"

"No," she said, "no, of course not." Talk about money always embarrassed her.

He laughed. "I guess the whole thing does sound kind of funny."

She would read that evening, on the back porch, and watch mosquitoes bump and buzz into the screen, and watch the big moths that came out every night for the moonflowers. If she got tired of that she could walk over to St. Charles Avenue and catch a streetcar and ride around the belt, making a big circle and getting off at her own stop forty minutes later. (It never occurred to her to call up any of the girls she knew—she did not particularly like them. She had never been too popular with men and since Fred was so obviously courting her, she got almost no calls for dates any more.)

"As a matter of fact," she said, "I'm not busy tonight."

She went straight from the phone to the bathroom and got out the special shampoo with the extra nice scent, the one she had been saving for the past two months. She rinsed her hair with vinegar to bring out the red lights, then shampooed and set it very carefully.

She went out in the back yard and sat in the sun to wait for it to dry.

She had been there an hour or so when her half-sister Doris came out. Joan shut her eyes and pretended she was asleep.

Doris came over and stood in front of her. "Come on. Quit pretending."

Joan opened her eyes and yawned. "I didn't hear you."

"The hell you didn't."

Doris was wearing a sweat-stained T shirt and a pair of dirty white shorts. They were as short as were allowed on the courts at Audubon Park.

She was taller than Joan and more slightly built. (They looked a good deal alike—more like full sisters than half-sisters—but then all the girls of the family favored their mother.) Joan was pretty in a conventional way: brown hair, blue eyes, fair skin that freckled in the sun. Doris was beautiful. She was blond, her short cropped hair bleached whitish by the sun and an occasional application of peroxide. Her face was rounder than her half-sister's, she had a cleft chin, and her nose was a smaller version of the sharp pinched Creole beak of her mother and sister.

She did not bother with make-up or lipstick in the mornings. Her tanned skin gleamed with sweat; it was flawless, not a blemish or a mark. Her eyes were heavily lashed and naturally shadowed. They were great lustrous brown eyes—just about the only things she had from her father, Raul Bringier. He had been a very handsome Cuban, and he had left Aurelie one day, saying simply that he was tired of speaking English all the time.

Joan thought with a twinge: she's golden and shiny, like a Christmas tree ornament.

"Come off it, old duck," Doris said.

"Make sense, will you."

"I hear you're going out with the great Michael Kern."

"He called," Joan said. "How did you know?"

"A little bird."

"Aurelie?"

"Sure."

She often listened on the upstairs extension. Joan had complained and screamed and ranted, but Aurelie had paid no attention. "It's an old habit, dear," she said simply. "From the time when I was married to Doris's father. I couldn't possibly get over it at my age now."

"She shouldn't have told you."

"Maybe she doesn't like date-stealers either."

"But he said he wasn't going with you any more," Joan lied. "He said you had a fight."

"I wouldn't be caught dead with that bastard."

"So what's the fuss?"

"Why do you think he called you?" Doris said. "Why the hell do you think he did that?"

Joan polished her nails with a calmness she did **not** feel. "Why does anybody call anybody?"

"He's doing it to show me," Doris said. "He wouldn't even look at you otherwise."

"Honestly," Joan said.

"You sneaky little bitch . . ." Doris's dark eyes slanted down. "If I wanted him you wouldn't get him."

"Don't be so dramatic, little sister."

For one moment she thought Doris would swing at her with the tennis racket she held in her left hand. But that moment passed, and Doris only gave a short vicious chop at a wasp that was drowsing on the top of the waxy white butterfly lilies. Then she stamped into the house.

HE was on time, almost to the minute. Joan was standing at the head of the stairs—she had been standing there motionless for at least five minutes—waiting for the bell. She went down slowly, setting her feet firmly, telling herself not to hurry or be flustered. And as she went, she realized that she didn't really remember what he looked like.

And if I don't even recognize him . . . I'll just die, she thought. That's all there is to it.

She stopped dead still on the bottom step. Her knees felt strange and she sat down.

And I just ironed the dress. . . .

The doorbell rang again. She got up and walked toward the door, her glance trailing along the floor. She noticed that where the polished boards met the wall there was a little layer of fluffy dust. Aurelie would have a fit if she saw that, she thought. It's strange that she didn't. She must be getting old. . . .

She recognized him at once. She would have known him anywhere. He was tall, but not very, and slight and small boned. He had black hair and fair skin and a very pronounced bluish beardline.

"Hi," she said, "you're the promptest man I've ever known."

"Can't help that."

"Come on in."

He hesitated, his hand on the door. "Why don't we go right on?"

Is it Doris he's thinking of? she wondered. Because he doesn't want to meet her? Or because he does and is afraid to?

But she only said: "I left my purse upstairs. I'll get it and be right back."

She went as quickly as she could in her heels on the polished floors. She gave her nose one dab with a puff, checked to be sure there was no lipstick on her teeth, then clattered down again.

He was snubbing out a cigarette in a standing pot of maidenhair fern.

He saw her glance. "The nicotine's good for them—I hope."

"I'm sure it is."

He had a Ford convertible, a few years old. "You want the top up?"

"No," she said, though she would have preferred it.

"That makes you a most unusual gal," he said, grinning. "Most would be screaming for it up before they stepped out of the house."

"I can comb my hair."

They drove through the heavy evening traffic until they got to the narrow bumpy road that led to the lake. He was very quiet; he seemed to be concentrating on his driving. As they were passing along the lake canal with its little protecting levees, she said finally, for want of anything else: "My grandfather built that."

He turned and looked at her. "Built what?"

"The canal."

"I thought soldiers built it during the Civil War."

"Are you sure?"

"Are you?"

The talk seemed so stupid to her suddenly that she wished she had kept quiet. "It's just a story they tell in my family," she said flatly. "That's all."

It was called Ruby's Place and it was built the way all Pontchartrain fishing camps were built—perched on thin tarred stilts over the shallow lake. A narrow white painted gangway led to the main building some hundred feet offshore. Joan and Michael walked along it slowly, squinting in the glare, listening to the steady gentle sucking of water beneath them, noticing how the creosoted pilings left thick layers of tar smell hanging in the air.

The camp was simply a platform with a roof,

wrapped around with screening. It held a single large room, filled with tables; the walls of a small kitchen cut across one corner. The floor boards banged and creaked uncertainly under their steps as they crossed to the west side to see the beginning of a sunset.

"It's going to be a lovely one," Joan said.

From this side of the camp another walk (without railings this time and just three boards wide) extended another hundred feet into the lake to a second platform set just above the water. This one was unscreened and empty, except for a clutter of wooden chairs and a few tables.

"Oh let's see out there," Joan said.

There was a strong fish odor to the platform, and the unpainted wood had been bleached and grained and warped by the sun.

"It's a swell place to catch crabs," Michael said. "Or neck."

"What would people do without the lake," she mocked gaily. He smiled back at her and she saw that this time she had got just exactly the right tone in her voice.

So that's how it's done, she thought; well, I can do that as well as anyone else. And his eyes crinkle up when he smiles.

"It would be easy to go in," she said.

"It's happened."

"To you?"

"Yes," he said. "I fell in once."

"What on earth were you doing?"

"Little lady," he said, "don't you go prying into my secret life."

She shrugged with elaborate carelessness. "Okay, man of mystery, buy me a beer."

They went back the narrow walk into the restaurant. Joan looked down at her feet following one another along the splintered boards. I could fall in too, she thought, but I won't let myself.

The room was almost empty. Only one group—three couples—sat laughing at a corner table. A shirt-sleeved waiter was tearing yesterday's date from the calendar that hung on the kitchen wall.

Michael steered her to the farthest table, one on the lake side, right at the edge. There was no railing there at all. The screen was simply tacked under the floor. They could look down directly into the muddy shivering water.

"Makes you think you're sitting right in it," Joan said. "Doesn't it?"

They had a beer or two and looked out across the empty expanse of lake. Once a boy went past in a battered skiff with a sputtering outboard on the stern. The ripples from his wake slapped against the pilings, briefly.

The sun went down in a yellow haze. "They must be burning prairie," she said.

"How can you tell?"

"Just looks like it."

The water turned a deep dusty orange. The camp was a growing black shadow on the little smooth waves. They pressed their noses against the screen, watching it lengthen and shift.

"I guess you know a lot about the city," he said.

"No, I don't."

"You're from here."

"Oh sure."

"Then you know. . . . Will you show me around some day?"

She felt a little pleasurable jolt. "It would be fun."

"We'll do it."

The crabs came, red from boiling and brown-streaked with the seasoning spices and heaped on a chipped black Falstaff-beer tray. He pulled one out, flipped it over, brushed off the bits of ice and handed it to her.

"Here," he said. "A present."

"Thanks."

"What's the matter?"

"Is it special?"

"It's a female."

She wondered if that was a joke of some sort. But she only said, "They taste alike."

"The roe, or the eggs or whatever you call it in crabs."

"You eat it?"

"Terrific—you never heard of that?"

She shook her head.

"Maybe you don't know so much about the city after all."

"I didn't say I did. That was your idea."

He took the crab back.

"And if you want a guide," she said huffily, "go down in the French Quarter and hire one."

He whistled through a crab leg. "What a temper!"

She didn't know what to think. And all of a sudden she remembered Fred and wondered if she would have to tell him that she had gone out with somebody else. And if she should tell him that it hadn't been any fun and that she had wondered about him and wished she were home. . . .

And him, he was laughing across the table. With the crabs and their dead black eyes staring at her.

He had said something to her—she had not heard it.

She folded her hands in her lap and said formally: "You think it is all very funny, but I am very sorry I came."

He tossed the shell down into a pail on the floor and took a swallow of beer. "How come?"

"I am mostly sorry because I don't know what to tell my fiancé."

"Look," he said, "I've never raped anybody in my life."

"You don't understand at all. I want to go home."

He studied her levelly. She wondered if her voice did not carry a note of conviction.

"Don't sound like a very silly schoolgirl." He grinned at her, a wonderful wide grin that made his eyes crinkle and his ears move.

She found herself smiling back, a little shyly at first. And then they were both laughing. Her purse slipped from her lap and into the shell pail. He got down on his hands and knees and pulled it out, stained and with little pepper seeds sticking to it.

He scrubbed at it with his napkin, then went back into the kitchen and worked at it with soap and water.

It was dark when they left. She stumbled, her heel caught in one of the uneven boards. He took her arm, steadying her.

"Watch," he said. "We can't ruin the dress too."

He held her arm tightly, his knuckles just grazing her breast. His hand stayed there until they got to the road. Then he dropped it and walked a few steps ahead to open the car door. He did not touch her again and she decided that it had been an accident.

He did not ask if she wanted to go home. He seemed to have forgotten that she had said it.

"Do you like jazz?" he asked.

"Grew up on it," she said gaily, thankful for the dark. She never lied well. Aurelie had considered jazz something for the kitchen and the tourist-filled stretches of Bourbon Street. Her girls were brought up on Tchaikovsky and Ravel.

"I thought we'd try the Red House over in Gretna."

"Sure." She had heard of that, of course. Doris had told her all about it.

"Dick Wilson is there."

She knew that name too, again from Doris. Why, she wondered, have I never gone there?

"I think that would be fun."

Perhaps something in her tone made him wonder. "You been there often before?"

"Not very often."

"It's nice," he said.

"I know that."

It was a big barn of a place, crowded even on weekday nights. They had to park two blocks away, at the edge of a deep drainage canal.

"I bet the kids catch crawfish there in the spring," Joan said.

"I don't know," Michael said. "I hate crawfish. . . . Look like roaches to me.

"Oh," Joan said, "sorry."

The closer they got to the building, the thicker the tangle of cars. Sometimes they had to retrace their steps because their way was blocked by cars bumper to bumper. Next to a white Mercury two men were having a violent argument over hooked fenders. As they passed, Michael whispered to her, "Can you understand a word?"

"Yes," Joan said. The staccato nasal speech was pleasant and familiar.

"For God's sake."

"Just Cajun French."

"Oh sure," Michael said. "I forgot about your mother."

"So did I," Joan said softly.

The people at the door seemed to know him, and Joan caught the little sidelong glances that were directed at her. They are comparing me to the other girls he's brought in here, she thought.

"You come in here a lot, don't you?"

"Not a lot," he said, "but a little."

They pushed their way inside to a table. Very soon Joan's ears began to sting from the unaccustomed blare. The music was very loud and almost continuous.

Every fifteen minutes—regular as a metronome—the band stopped. They got up, stretched and scratched, mopped their foreheads and shouldered their instruments. The second band was already climbing up. There was a brief silence while they arranged themselves.

In the interval Joan and Michael exchanged a few crisp, disjointed words, hastily.

"Watch the piano," Michael told her once, "he's terrific."

And every now and then, while the band belted out a piece, he would learn over and tap her arm, calling her attention to some particular aspect of the performance. She always nodded back, trying to look knowing, actually having not the slightest idea what he was telling her.

They said very little. During the brief intermissions Michael usually dashed off to get more bottles of beer. While the band played, he sat hunched over the table, frowning with the effort of concentration. The music was far too loud to talk over anyhow.

"I used to want to play like that," he told her almost an hour later. "Want another beer?"

She shook her head. He did not get one for himself. He seemed to have had enough; he seemed to have stopped drinking abruptly.

"You know," he smiled a crooked little smile, "all through high school and college I was crazy to play with a band."

"Why didn't you?"

He shook his head. She noticed that there was a little white trace of beer foam on his lip. "I don't know why," he said. "I wish I had, but there's no living in that."

"They seem to be making a living." She nodded toward the band.

"They all have other jobs in the daytime," he said. "Work like dogs."

"Oh," she said.

"I couldn't do that, so I didn't try. . . . Just sometimes I wish I had."

The band began again, and he slumped forward into his listening crouch.

Joan was wondering if she should suggest going somewhere else—and wondering how she could do that—when he said abruptly, in one of the brief spells of quiet: "Let's go."

I've not had a chance to talk to him at all, she thought. But he didn't seem to want to say anything.

She chattered on the way home, gaily, as Aurelie had trained her to do. He took her to the front steps—up the brick walk and past the tile fountain—and through the open windows she heard the little porcelain clock on the hall mantel striking eleven. Then she understood.

She held out her hand. "Thank you very much," she said, mechanically, "it was a very pleasant evening."

"And you'll take me sight-seeing one day?"

"Not now, anyhow," she said; "you haven't got time. After all, it's eleven, and you can't be too late, even to a late date."

Her back was to the light, and the soft glow, filtered through the lead glass, showed his face distinctly. So that she saw the quick flicker of surprise, the little start of guilt.

She laughed out loud. A few feet away the little fountain seemed to echo her. "Dear boy," she said in a clear imitation of Aurelie, "you didn't think I didn't know, did you?"

The flicker was gone. He recovered himself quickly. "You're a witch," he said gently.

"Do have a splendid time, dear boy. . . ."

And she slipped inside the door, closing it firmly behind her.

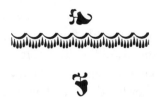

3

THE hall looked the way it always did at night. The mahogany table and the two carved lion's-head chairs were black and massive in the small yellow light from the bronze lamp with the fringed shade. That lamp was so hideous—she had always hated it. It had had bead fringe once, and one rainy afternoon when she was a small girl—five or six or so—she had carefully worked away at it until the tiny glass beads were all pulled off and scattered to the corners of the room. When Aurelie saw it, she shrieked and clutched at her breast so that the little Joan began to laugh hysterically. Until Aurelie had taken her to the kitchen and spanked her—hard— with the fly swatter. (It wasn't a new one either, she remembered; there were still some black squashed flies imbedded in the screen wire.) Then Aurelie dragged her back into the hall and made her watch while she got a brush and pan and went over the room on hands and

44

knees, carefully collecting the beads. When she had done, and all the beads that were possibly there had been gathered up, she looked down at the small pile, mixed with dust in the pan, and shook her head sadly. There weren't nearly enough.

"You impossible child!" For a minute Joan clutched her rear, thinking that they were going back for the fly swatter. Then the anger in Aurelie's face changed slowly to horror. "You ate them," she said softly. "You must have." With a movement so fast that Joan was caught off balance, Aurelie grabbed her arm and carried her back to the kitchen. She forced her to swallow great hunks of soft white bread and drink glass after glass of water.

There had been a doctor too, Joan remembered, but not very vividly. Funny, she thought, the things she remembered best always had something to do with her mother. . . .

She went over and stood looking at the lamp closely. I still hate it, she said to herself, and wouldn't Aurelie be surprised if I pulled off all the fringe. . . .

They were becoming fashionable again, she had to admit. Like the horrible iridescent Tiffany bud vase that stood on Aurelie's dressing table. . . .

The good things are all down here or in Aurelie's room, she thought. But I wouldn't have them in mine. . . . As soon as I can spare the money I'll do my room all over in blond wood and mirrors and black lacquer tables.

And I wonder who he is having the late date with. . . .

Because it was an old habit, she went to the kitchen to see what was left in the icebox.

There was only one light on. It was enough for her to make out Doris and a boy leaning head to head across the little kitchen table under the window.

They did not move when she came in, but she felt their eyes roll over toward her. "Excuse me," Joan said, "but I was going to the icebox."

The heads separated. "Hi, old duck," Doris said in a vague voice. A tall thin blond boy stood up: "Good evening."

"You remember Charles, don't you," Doris said.

"Sure," Joan said, though she did not.

"This is my rich sister," Doris said.

"I'll just check the icebox and be right out," Joan said.

"We were fixing supper," Charles said. He sounded embarrassed.

Joan found a piece of cheese and the heel of a loaf of French bread. She got an orange from the bowl on the window and dumped them all together in a single plate.

"Did you have a fun time?" Doris asked in her softest most southern voice.

"No I didn't." Joan was surprised to find herself telling the truth. So she went on. "I see what you mean—he *is* a creep."

Doris's giggle followed her upstairs.

. . .

Aurelie was reading a magazine in the tiny study at the head of the stairs. She had done her hair up high on her head and tied it with a green ribbon, and she wore a taffeta housecoat that rustled with each breath she took. The wallpaper of patterned green roses, the Victorian chairs of dark mahogany and rosewood were soft and muted and motherly.

Aurelie looked over the top of her magazine, and the taffeta rustled more loudly. "And how was your stolen tryst?"

"I wish everybody would just lay off me," Joan said.

"My dear child . . ."

"Will you please get Doris to stop calling me her rich sister?"

"My child, my child," Aurelie said melodramatically, "only two of my girls at home, and they can't get on."

"Oh shit!"

"I need not tell you what I think of that expression."

"I can't help it," Joan said, "I get that from my father."

"Your father," Aurelie said, and pulled off her glasses to polish them on her hem, "was extremely quiet and soft spoken."

"He was a gambler and a crook," Joan persisted. "If he hadn't died right when he did, he'd have gone to Atlanta prison with all those other people."

"Such a quiet dull man." Aurelie was speaking gently to herself. "Who would have thought he'd be such a very terribly dull man."

"Tell me one thing," said Joan. "Did you marry him because he was rich?"

"Honestly, child . . ."

"Why else?"

"He was a most intriguing man," Aurelie said, "from a distance."

Joan remembered him so clearly she couldn't believe he'd been dead ten years. A short chunky man, a blond Italian from Lombardy. A nervous man, a restless man with a heart damaged by rheumatic fever. And his parents, staid respectable shopkeepers, shocked by their son's emigration. And shocked again by his change of name. During one of the summers Joan had spent with him (long after the divorce; the marriage had lasted only a few months after her birth) he had showed her a letter from them, a letter in fine cramped writing. He had been chuckling, she remembered. "The old people," he'd told her, "how can you explain to them? Even twenty years later they are worrying about this because they don't understand—a new country, a new name. Anthony Mitchell sounds good, little one." That same summer, she remembered, he'd had a playhouse built for her, a tiny perfect house, furnished with tiny furniture and with a stove and an icebox that actually worked. He met her there every afternoon, and they walked up to the main house and had supper together, him watching, whisky in hand, while she ate. Sometimes there would be someone else there too, if he happened to have a friend staying with him. . . . That particular summer Joan thought it had been a tall beautiful woman named Margaret. She had never known her last name, she only called her Margaret. It seemed to her sometimes that Margaret had been around more than the others; maybe he was even going to marry her. But he hadn't; and a couple of years later he was dead. Then all there was left was in Metairie Cemetery, a fancy marble tomb with two angels and a cross and the name Anthony Mitchell carved across the front of it, in letters a foot high. . . .

Aurelie's taffeta rustled and Joan was twenty again and back in the house on Coliseum Street.

"Doesn't it seem funny to you," Joan asked, "all of us living on his money?"

"He was most generous."

"Just that fountain, why do you suppose he was so crazy about that fountain?"

"I was in love with him," Aurelie said, "or I would never have let him put it there."

"Why did he want to keep it so very much?"

"I haven't the faintest idea, child."

"You know what?" Joan asked, "I know why he didn't marry Margaret. I think he was still in love with you."

Aurelie shrugged. "Such a quiet dull man."

That was the only comment she had ever made.

Joan chuckled. The nasty taste of the evening with Michael was disappearing; she was feeling better.

Aurelie went back to her magazine.

"You know," Joan said, "you look so wonderfully motherly, with glasses, I mean."

"I've heard about bifocal contact lenses," Aurelie said without lifting her eyes from the page, "I shall have to see about them."

JOAN had her hand on the door to her room when the phone rang. Michael's *calling back*. . . .

She waited, holding her breath. But she was still not surprised when she heard Aurelie begin a conversation.

It couldn't be. But if it was, I'd have gone out and waited for him.

She went into her room.

And he'll never come back. Because I wasn't the sort of girl he likes. . . .

She'd felt this way before. The ache was familiar. Hurt pride, she told herself scornfully. Why do I have to get so upset just because my little pride gets hurt? All these feelings, all these god-damn feelings. . . .

It's something about me, she thought. I never can get the men I want.

She felt sad. Very sad. And being sad felt good. It was a pleasure, really. Like eating something you liked. A mild pleasure. The whole world took on a lovely grey tinge and everything was weeping.

She dragged the record player and its little table across the room and plugged it in right beside the bed. Then she rummaged around in the back of her closet until she found the recording she wanted: *Liebestod*.

She lay back on the bed and closed her eyes and thought great cloudy thoughts and felt sadness run over her in huge predictable waves like the surf.

Every now and then she spoke out loud to herself. "It's hell to be alive," she told herself, "and it would be hell to be dead too." The record finished. Without getting up she lifted the arm and started it over again, turning up the volume. "If I died, they would be sorry." And she saw herself laid out.

"I don't get anything right. Not ever."

She put the record on for a third time and cried little fat tears into the hot still night.

AURELIE insisted on breakfast, a formal breakfast in the dining room. The table was carefully set with the same flower-patterned spode each morning. The food was carefully arranged on the buffet over little warmers and under little covers.

It was the one rule of the house. Aurelie said nothing about late hours, never had. From the time they left the nursery and moved into rooms of their own, her daughters came and went as they pleased. But each and every morning, they were required to appear for breakfast. Aurelie, her hair carefully arranged, her face carefully made up, her robe of crisp taffeta in the summer and soft velvet in the winter, sat at the head of the table and made polite cheery conversation.

These mornings, as for a good many years past, Aurelie was alone. Her husband Herbert Norton had long since stopped coming down. (Her previous husband, and the only other one Joan had been old enough to remember, had never been present in the mornings either.

He had been a tall thin Lincoln-like Alabamian, a hard-working surgeon, who was always up at five thirty, out of the house by six, and operating by seven.)

For the first year of their marriage Herbert Norton had appeared for breakfast. Or rather Aurelie had gone up and brought him down. Joan remembered his big nearsighted blue eyes circled by gold-rimmed glasses, peering out from behind Aurelie as they entered the room. He was much taller than she was; he was very nearly six feet, but he gave the impression of being small. He was delicate-boned and thin, formally polite and very self-effacing. He had been in the Navy for twenty years, had married Aurelie and retired. That had been ten years past. For those years he had drunk steadily, seriously. Whenever Aurelie went for him, he was most polite and came most willingly. But he had to be fetched for each appearance, and after a few years Aurelie no longer bothered. So, bit by bit, he disappeared: first from the breakfast table, then from the main part of the house and the main part of their lives. Some three years after their marriage Aurelie had the top floor, the third floor, remodeled for him. He had insisted on only one thing: a fire escape, an ugly old-fashioned iron one, that climbed the side of the house. After that he seemed quite happy to move up there. By then it had been months since they had gone out together, and when Aurelie entertained at home, she often forgot to fetch him. After all, he had no friends and seemed rather glad to be left alone.

He did not come down at all. Aurelie's cook brought him his meals. And there was a phone that he used only to call the liquor store.

He did not even seem to be particularly interested in his daughter, Ann. Just a year after the marriage Aurelie had borne another daughter, a thin dark baby with tilted eyes and pointed pixie ears, who turned into a tall thin precocious child with a startling resemblance to Aurelie and none at all to her father. She spent her summers at camp and her winters at convent school in Florida.

Most of the time Joan forgot he was in the house, remembering only when she saw the delivery boy from the liquor store climbing up the three flights, cursing softly under his breath. Remembering again when the doctor plodded up wearily, for Mr. Norton had had two mild heart attacks.

Every evening with the gathering dark he pulled in the shutters and closed all the windows in his two rooms and locked them. And every morning with the first strong light—four thirty in the summers and seven in the winters—he staggered around opening them again. At the one that was framed by the highest shoots of the moonflower vine he would always stop, press his nose against the screen and take a couple of deep breaths. The dust on the screen invariably made him sneeze, a gigantic snort that echoed all along the block. Each morning it was the same. The people in the house had gotten so used to it that they no longer even heard it.

He lived peacefully up there, with his charts and military books and strange old-fashioned navigating instruments. And every now and then he made a trip to the hospital to have his gentle little delusions replaced by heavy shots of vitamin B.

His stepdaughters forgot he was there. And if Aurelie remembered, she never mentioned it.

So, that morning, the third of June, only Aurelie and Doris were at the table when Joan came down.

Aurelie glanced at her critically. "Mercy sakes, child," she said to Joan when she appeared, "whatever happened to your eyes?"

"Nothing happened to them."

Doris, who was wearing clean white shorts and a shirt, grinned over her coffee cup. "Wagner all night long, huh?"

"Honestly," Aurelie said, "were you playing that again?"

Joan shrugged and poured her coffee. "I happen to like music."

"I'll forgive you," Doris said. "You want to come play tennis?"

"Where's your date?"

"I've got one, honey, don't you worry. But I was going to ask him to bring a friend for you."

"Thanks," Joan said, "but my tennis isn't very good."

"You've got to do something here in the summer."

"I think," Joan said, "I'll go take a course." She enjoyed their surprise. And the plan grew as she spoke. "A cultural summer. I'm going to sign up for a couple of courses in music over at the college."

"Good old tone deaf," Doris said.

"Honestly, child," Aurelie said, "what a waste of money."

"It's my money," Joan said stubbornly, "and I can spend it any way I want."

"That," Doris said, "reminds me of a joke."

"Not at breakfast," Aurelie said.

"Wouldn't you think you'd get enough school all year without adding to it in the summer?"

"That's my affair."

"Okay, rich bitch," Doris said.

"That is quite enough," Aurelie said.

"It's nice," Doris said, "to have an intellectual sister."

"A bookish woman," Aurelie said, "is simply impossible."

"Call my broker," Doris mimicked, "I am just loaded with money."

Joan stared at the blue glass Victorian jam jar and the silver napkin ring that lay beside it. "Two of you," she said slowly. And she picked up the ring and balanced it on the top of the jam jar. "The two of you line up against me."

"Ohhhhhh," Doris moaned, "poor little meeeeee."

"Oh child," Aurelie said, "you are so solemn."

Joan studied the edge of the plate, and slowly she

went over every object on the table as if she had never seen them before. "The two of you," she repeated. And the words brought back the sorrow of last night, the wonderful lovely sorrow. . . . The lost . . . the something that was lost, the place you couldn't go back to, the dream you didn't want to give up in the morning and you lay tight in bed trying and trying to hold it and it slipped away, like fog, and you couldn't remember the smell or the color or the feel of it, what it was and where it had been. And that was the final end, when there wasn't even a memory. . . .

Joan lifted her eyes in time to see Doris clutching her throat in anguish, chanting: "Oh woe, oh woe, O *Weltschmerz*, O *Wiener Schnitzel*, O crap, O shit."

Aurelie brought her palm down on the table sharply so that the dishes rattled. "That is quite enough. Leave the table."

"Yes, Mother. Going, Mother. Right away, Mother." Doris giggled, but she got up at once and slipped out of the door into the kitchen. They could hear her begin a conversation with the cook. In a couple of minutes a car tooted outside, and the kitchen door slammed. The car zoomed off, double clutching with a roar.

Aurelie poured herself some coffee, then filled Joan's cup. "Here, you funny little sad thing," she said.

Joan added sugar without answering.

"One thing . . ." Aurelie said, "my daughters are different. Joan, honey, don't you think you'd be happier if you were married?"

"Fred?"

"A very fine man," Aurelie said. "I couldn't approve more. And we haven't had a lawyer in this family for generations."

"I think I'll go to medical school and never get married."

Aurelie chuckled her deep mannish tones. "You flunked biology, dear."

"I might be a missionary."

"A nice man," Aurelie said. "We've been so unlucky with men in this family."

"Your favorite subject," Joan said sourly.

"A woman alone," Aurelie said, "is so very sad."

"If I'm going to register," Joan said, "I've got to get dressed and over there."

She felt her mother's accusing eyes follow her from the room.

SHE had been in college for two years and it seemed just like another school day as she walked the short three blocks from the front gate on Coliseum Street to the campus. At the first corner she pulled an orange hibiscus from the bush in the Landry yard, the way she did every morning. For the rest of that block, without looking, she tore the saucer-shaped flower to careful pieces so that she left an orange trail behind her. At the second corner she stopped on the iron walk that crossed the gutter and dropped in the last bits of stamen and green leaf that her fingers still held. It was a deep gutter, its sides lined with careful sloping slabs of slate. Since it was the deepest drain in the neighborhood there was always water in it—even once when it had frozen (back when she was a child of six or seven) there had been ice so thick on it that the children had come down and walked along it, making skating motions. Until Philip Carter, the redheaded boy who lived two blocks away,

went home and got his roller skates. After a couple of
trips he had cut through the ice and the wheels had
wedged in the soft mud. That was the end of the ice
skating. By afternoon the sun slipped around under the
trees and the ice melted. There had not been another
freeze like that again. For weeks after there was the
smell of dead foliage decaying in the sun.

At the third corner a streetcar went clanking past and
she stopped and sniffed its peculiar smell, sharp and
pungent and exciting. As if it were reminding her always that she was about to leave for a marvelous
place. . . .

She loved the streetcars. Each time the city removed
a line she felt a little clutch of bewilderment; she could
see the day coming when there would be no more left.
And what then? And where would she go then when she
was disturbed and sick with the peculiar kind of nausea
that fear gave her? . . .

She was afraid of so many things. Sometimes for no
reason at all, she would feel the muscles knot up and the
cold feeling begin. Then she would head for the streetcar line and ride, back and forth, for an hour or so, until
the noisy rocking ride comforted her.

She stared after the car as it traveled rapidly down the
tracks, rocking decidedly from side to side, a clumsy cat-
erpillar-shaped creature.

It was nice to have it there. . . .

She was whistling as she turned through the imitation Gothic gates that bore a bronze plaque saying

A Gift of the Class of 1905. She noticed that one of the little lamps had a broken glass.

She had never been to summer school before, but she had not expected any difference. When she came around the building and looked out over the quadrangle, she stopped abruptly, startled, trying to see what had changed.

It wasn't the people. There were as many of them as ever, streaming over to the far building to register for their classes. It was the grounds. They looked seedy— like a good suit that had been slept in.

Under the fierce June sun and the heavy rains, the staff of gardeners made no headway. There was one man now, an enormously fat Negro, wheeling about on a tremendous lawn mower. He flicked by her. Grass splattered out on the path. She studied the cut blades and fancied that she could see them begin to grow again, leaping up from under the path of the mower.

You could feel it growing, she thought, even under the pavement.

The bed of zinnias had gone wild, too. They grew at right angles to the ground, like mad children crawling along on hands and knees. Next to a building a single sunflower shot straight up and turned its flat yellow face at the level of the second-floor windows, ten feet high. And the honeysuckle, along the walls, sprouted long wavy arms into the air or stuck creeping exploring fingers along the brick.

A girl and a young man went by, holding hands

loosely in the heat. Her full starched petticoats and skirt rustled and left a faint trail of starch smell. Joan found herself watching after them, watching the girl's feet, lean brown feet in tiny-strapped white sandals.

I've got ugly feet, she thought, thin and long and bony. My toes are funny lengths and the veins go back and forth, like clotheslines. I wish I had nice feet and I wouldn't have to wear stockings and cover-up shoes all the time. . . .

She walked along toward the registration building. A wasp droned over her head and a tremendous green grasshopper flashed across her path. Out of sight, but not far off, a Good Humor man went past, his wagon tinkling a distorted version of the Brahms Lullaby. A large brown and white dog loped up and began digging frantically in a camellia bed. When the hole was deep and long enough, he curled around in it, fitting it to himself, and stretched out, belly down on the cool damp.

Joan was watching him, when from behind her some-one said: "Of all the people I didn't expect to find in summer school, you are it."

She went on watching the dog. The voice was familiar; she had heard it before, but she could not place it. If I turn around, she told herself just as slowly as she could think, I could tell who it is. . . . If I turn around. . . .

It was a thing she did, this thinking very slowly. She worked at it; she had trained herself so that thoughts came before her mind in a sleepy progression. She had chance to turn each one over and study it, like the slow progression of slides under a microscope.

"I was saying hello." Michael Kern stepped around and stood directly in front of her. "Hello again."

"I don't like to be hurried," she said stupidly.

His eyes were a yellowish brown, she noticed, in the strong sun.

"So take your time."

The slow progression was ruined. Things speeded up to their ordinary pace. She felt annoyed and cheated.

"What are you taking?" she asked.

"Taking?" He could lift one eyebrow straight up so that it almost touched his low growing hair. "I'm giv-ing."

"You're what?"

"I teach," he said. "Didn't Doris tell you?"

She wished he had not said that, and wished that the words had not made a difference.

"I don't think we talked about it."

"Didn't she say anything about me?"

"Why should she?"

"Didn't you want to know what I did when you went out with me?"

"No," she said. "It didn't seem important. At all."

"For God's sake."

She began to walk toward the building. He fell into step beside her.

"You're a strange gal."

"I suppose I should ask what you teach?"

"No, honey bunch," he said, "but it's economics."

"Oh."

"Take my course."

"I'm taking art this summer. Art survey."

"Why?"

"Something to do. The summers are kind of long if you don't do something."

"What did you take last year?"

"I didn't," she said. "I went to Jamaica and then to Mexico."

"Sounds like fun."

"So much fun I can't afford to go back this year."

"That's a shame."

"Not really."

They passed the cafeteria. "Want a cup of coffee?"

"No," she said, "I'd rather go and get finished right now."

"Okay," he said, "see you." He touched her shoulder briefly.

The registration hall was stifling. She stood in endless lines and waited patiently, staring at the sweat-stained shirts around her, seeing them and not really seeing them. The tall Gothic windows on each side were open, but no breeze moved through them. Mosquitoes came, in slow drifting clouds and dragonflies followed them, weaving back and forth with quick ducking movements. Outside, and far off, the band began practice, the summer band, sounding thin and reedy. Most of the players would have gone home.

She sat down on the floor in a corner and patiently filled out a long duplicate form, writing laboriously on the back of her purse. She paid little attention to what she was doing. Her eyes without looking were observing, and her ears were listening.

In the heat the smell of sex was almost tangible, almost hung in the air like smoke. She noticed that at the beginning of every term—men and women thrown together in the same large hall, brushing elbows, brushing hips, until the air was full and you could almost hear the heavy breathing. She had always noticed that. The glance, the appraisal—she hated the girls for their coy peep from under the lashes; she knew what they were thinking. She knew what Doris was thinking. Doris liked to talk and had explained in great detail what she looked for in a man, how she selected him first, from across a room, and what she liked in bed.

And no one, she thought, is trying me. . . . That was the way it always happened. She was nice looking, she was even quite pretty; she had a lovely figure, lush and full. But there was something in her that repelled advances. She wondered about that. She even knew what it was, but not how to change it.

A certain directness, a businesslike manner, that was not very feminine. A manner that reminded of tweeds and low-heeled shoes and sensible hats. . . . She looked a great deal like Elizabeth of England; people told her that often.

She thought with a wry smile: that means I look more motherly than wifely. . . .

She had almost finished filling the registration form. She had come to the part that asked for her religious preference. Always before this she had written Catholic. Though she had not been in a church for years.

This time, she wrote plainly: Mahayana Buddhist.

That would interest them, she thought, if they ever bothered to read those things.

The idea amused her. She stopped writing and grinned out across the crowded floor.

As she did, she caught a brief glimpse of Michael Kern. Or perhaps it wasn't. But it was enough. For all the rest of the morning she could feel the imprint of his hand on her shoulder.

THE June days slipped one into the other. Doris won the city's singles tennis championship. She and Aurelie argued for days about having the trophy in the living room. Aurelie won, as she always did. Doris carried the hideous yellow thing up to her room and sulked.

Fred Aleman went on his two-week vacation. Joan saw him off on the cruise ship at the Julia Street wharf, the sleek white ship that would eventually deposit him at Buenos Aires. She brought him a little box of English cookies, a hideous tin box with a leering picture of Winston Churchill on the cover in four garish colors. She kissed him good bye awkwardly, wondering if anyone was looking. And clumped down the gangplank, catching her heel and almost tripping, conscious suddenly that her white dress had a smear of black tar. . . .

The other days blended together in a mist of heat and steamy rains. She went to class, sat and listened and wrote down the parts of a symphony and the definition of a fugue and bought herself a recorder and practiced on it at night.

After about a week the assistant dean asked to see her. He was a short balding young man, with an apoplectic face and a heavy mood of jollity that was a protection against student problems.

"Now what do we have here?" he laughed mirthlessly.

Joan felt silly. "I don't know," she said, "what do we have?"

He looked at her sharply.

"I wasn't being funny," she said.

"Sign up for a course in art and then don't appear. . . . The instructor is wondering what happened to you."

He held out the class card. Joan took it and studied it slowly. There, in her own handwriting. Two courses listed: the music, then Art 103.

She remembered. "I'm sorry."

"Haven't been sick?"

"No," she said.

"You don't want to change to another course or anything like that?"

"No," she said again. "I just forgot I had registered for this."

"You what?"

"Forgot. I just forgot."

"Well, well," he muttered with heavy irony, "the heat does strange things to all of us."

"I know that sounds silly."

"Do you think," he said, standing up, "you could manage to remember now?"

"Yes," she answered seriously. "Yes, I can."

"It might be a splendid thing to do."

"I will," she said, "yes, I will. And thank you for reminding me."

He stopped the reply that was balanced on his tongue. She probably didn't mean that. As they shook hands, he studied her eyes carefully. They were nice eyes, blue, with dark lashes. They had a sick look too; they were sort of opaque. So he kept still and only allowed himself to sigh, deep and sad, after she had gone. "We get them all," he said aloud as he went over to the window and checked to be sure that the air conditioner was really working at full capacity.

Joan went to art class the very next day. And found she liked it. She bought herself a pale green smock and spent hours scratching away with pieces of charcoal on large pads of white paper. She took her sketches home and pinned them to the wall with tiny bits of Scotch tape. After two weeks most of the great pink cabbage roses were hidden from sight.

Aurelie, who never came to her room, slipped in the door one day and looked around. "Mercy, child," she said, "this is such a strange summer."

"Who told you?" Joan demanded. "Who told you about them? That little bitch Doris?"

"How sharper than a serpent's tooth it is to have a thankless child," Aurelie quoted.

"Oh shit!"

"The lack of range in your vocabulary," Aurelie said, "is simply appalling."

"God," Joan said, "don't you ever get angry?"

"A soft answer turneth away wrath."

"Oh God," Joan said.

The following week, which was just a few days before Fred came home, Joan got a job at the college library. From four until eleven at night, when the library closed, she sat up on the sixth level of the stacks at a hard little steel desk and waited for circulation to call for books on that floor.

Nobody wanted that job. It was the next to the highest level and the air conditioning didn't work too well up there, so there was always the stuffy odor of gently moving dust and the faintly carbolic odor of the bindings. It was the quietest of all the levels. There were few calls for books and hardly anyone came by. The staff had always tossed coins for it, until Joan came.

She liked it up there. Liked the dusty quiet. Liked the emptiness. And sometimes she went up to the next level, the highest level, where there were no windows at all, only faint yellow bulbs too small to cast much light. Uncatalogued things were kept there. Heaps of old magazines. Wooden boxes of mementos. And collections given to the library as units. The smell of old leather was as thick as incense. Pictures. And daguerreotypes. And swords in velvet boxes. One small wood box labeled Souvenirs of Sarah Bernhardt. Joan would have opened that, but the top was nailed on. She pried at it some with a little fingernail file she carried in her purse but gave it up to open a hand-bound volume of ornate leather called *The Genealogy of the Wives of Louisiana Governors.*

Because her heels echoed so on the glass floor, she took to leaving her shoes under the desk and padding silently about the top level in her nylons. There was a single window on the west side, and she discovered it one day. After that she would spend hours standing there, leaning against the concrete, looking out over the campus. She was above even the tops of the trees and she felt floating and detached. The window didn't open, so she could hear no sounds; she only saw the play of light, the changing from day to evening, from evening to dark. The evening star would swim into view just over the biggest of the oak trees. She would see the lights come on, yellow for some, blue for the fluorescents.

There were some rooms on the south side of the level, little empty rooms all in a line, like the tiny rooms in an army hospital. They were windowless too with only a big round O of fluorescent tube in the ceiling. On their doors, right under the small clear glass square of window looking in, was a carefully lettered sign: Study. It was done in very precise Gothic script.

The rooms were not used, never had been. Their concrete brick walls were not even painted. No one came up here. She like to go into the rooms sometimes and stand very still and listen and try to imagine things or remember things, she was never sure which. She was only sure that it was very important for her to do it.

She would turn on the overhead corridor light (only one worked) and stare at the dust as it floated under it.

One evening, after supper, and shortly before the library closed, she was padding around as usual in her bare feet. There had been a couple of calls for books, only one of which she had been able to find. She circled aimlessly looking for the remaining one, the call slip clutched in her hand.

She was passing back by the line of studies when she noticed the noise. Not a real sound so much as a brushing. A sound that almost wasn't a sound.

Instinct told her sharply: go back to the desk and read; you haven't heard anything. But she padded silently along. It was the second little square glass window she looked into. The door was almost closed and the window was coated with grime, but still she had no trouble making out the two figures on the floor.

For a long second she watched, scarcely realizing what she was seeing, thinking with silly precision: the floor must be awful on their backs. . . . Then she felt the delayed rush of embarrassment and scooted back to her desk. She sat for a moment under the little gooseneck lamp, studying the scratched initials on the metal top. Then she put on her shoes and pounded down the narrow stairs to the next level.

"Hi," she said, "I got lonesome so I thought I'd come down and say hello."

The three girls who worked that level stared at her in surprise. She had never done that before.

FRED ALEMAN came back, his olive skin tanned almost mahogany by wind and sun. He brought Joan a vicuña stole and a long necklace—a marriage chain, he called it—of silver so soft she could bend it in her fingers. Joan folded the stole away to wait for cool weather and wore the necklace dutifully each time she went out with him.

She saw him only on week ends now, on the nights she didn't work at the library. She wondered sometimes if the change in their plans had upset him, but he said nothing. He did call her every evening when she got home. But if he missed her he said nothing.

One Saturday—the first since he'd come back—he took her to the concert in Beauregard Square. She wore a brand-new blue print dress, cut low in back, and she had borrowed Aurelie's beaded bag. Fred's cluster of tiny white roses perched on her shoulder. They sat in the warm still night, at a table that was too small, and drank rum collinses. Her stockings snagged on a splintered chair. The unmoving air still smelled heavily of the DDT with which the area had been sprayed. Even so, a few mosquitoes circled and droned lazily overhead.

"Do you remember," Joan said, "how often we used to come to these last summer?"

"I think it was a better series last year," Fred said.

"And how we used to go out to the lake at night and go swimming?"

"And how you thought you saw a gar?"

She made a face. "I did feel something. . . . But all that was fun."

"Yes," he said, "it was."

If he would only tell her. If he would only admit that he missed her those weekday evenings. She wondered what he did, though she knew she should never ask. Maybe he was finding somebody else. She didn't even know if he missed her.

"I get to thinking about it sometimes," she admitted slowly. "And it was kind of fun when we had time to go and do things like that."

He leaned back in the chair, which creaked under his weight, and chuckled. "Young lady," he said, "if you didn't want to work evenings, you wouldn't do it. And wild horses couldn't drag you there."

She smiled feebly. He still hadn't said.

She watched him in the little light from the one candle on the table. He was handsome, in a heavy solid way. The thick black hair, the heavy jaw, the wide forehead.

"You know," she said, "what's the best thing about you?"

"No," he said. "What?"

"Your coloring. Olive skin and black eyes are awfully good with a white shirt."

"Thank you, ma'am."

Then it popped out. "What do you do in the evenings, when I'm working?"

He smiled gently. "Layovers to catch meddlers."

"No," she said, "I mean it."

"So do I."

His smile wasn't as gentle as she had first thought. But she plunged ahead, because she had gone too far to stop. "I just wanted to know."

"What do you do?"

"I work."

"I've heard."

"I haven't been chasing around with anybody."

"I didn't think so, but I'm glad to hear it."

"Do you?"

"I told you: layovers to catch meddlers."

He was teasing now, and she stopped, knowing that she had brought up a subject that would spoil the rest of the evening. He was annoyed with her, she could tell. She had known him too long not to recognize the signs.

Why do I always do it, she thought fiercely. Why do I have to ruin things? Why always me? And I still don't know if he misses me. I don't even know that.

"I'm sorry," she said miserably and then saw that the

apology had made things worse; it had embarrassed him. She stared down at her glass and busily removed a gnat that had fallen in.

"When this is finished," he said, "want to go out to the Fairfax Club and try your luck?"

It was an old joke between them. She had never been able to bring herself to gamble. She would go and stand by the tables by the hour and watch the players and watch the wheel and the board or the dice. She would go to the races and study the form and dope out the horses and head toward the parimutuel window, but somehow she always came back with the money jammed way down in the pocket of her coat. She couldn't do it. Not even just two dollars.

"I'd like to go," she said truthfully. The sense of excitement in the gamblers about her always left her exhilarated too.

"When the concert's over," Fred promised.

"It's not really very good tonight."

"I'm afraid not."

"It's not nearly as good as last year," she said.

Hours later they went into the bar at the Fairfax Club. It was deserted, as it nearly always was. Most people preferred the gambling rooms.

Joan sat at the bar, swishing out her skirts so that they did not get mussed. She put Aurelie's little beaded handbag on the bar and folded her gloves neatly on top.

"Why is it always empty in here?"

"I suppose," Fred said, "most people want to be near the action."

"Oh." She noticed the clock, twenty past one. That was why she felt tired.

"You get to play tonight?"

"Don't tease me, Fred."

He grinned. "A wild gambler like you, always after the action. . . ."

"I saw you play," she said hastily. "Did you win?"

"Some," he said; "enough to buy our drinks anyway."

"I'm glad."

She ordered brandy and soda. He lifted his eyebrows but said nothing when the empty-eyed barman brought the soda and she poured it as a chaser.

"Don't look so disapproving."

"My dear child," he said, "your drinking is not one of the things I worry about."

She thought she had an opening then, a faint one, and she pushed right ahead, wondering if she was going to have it now. "What do you worry about?"

"About you?" he laughed softly. "Not very much. You're a smart gal, with a sensible mother, so who can worry?"

That wasn't it, she thought. It took a turn the wrong way and went off where I didn't want it to go, and I can't bring it back. Where was it? It was there. Somewhere. And I lost it.

He was speaking to her, still teasing. "Of course I might worry about your gambling."

She finished her brandy, and twirled the empty glass. The barman came over and she pushed it to him. Fred nodded to him.

"Why do you suppose," Joan said, "that I can't gamble?"

"I don't know. Any ideas?"

"Maybe because my father was a gambler."

"Now you've gone Freudian on me."

"Did you ever know my father?"

"That's a funny thing to ask."

"Did you?"

"I met him, of course. Long before I knew you."

"How? How did you meet him?"

"We had business," Fred said. "When he was selling that big LaChaise tract out by the lake."

"Oh," she said.

"After all," he said, "you couldn't be around downtown very much and not run into him."

"I never saw him downtown," she said.

"He was sort of all over the place. I can still see him rushing off down the corridor, with his heels going like drums on the marble."

"I never saw him there," she repeated; "I only used to see him when I went across the Tickfaw on week ends and holidays."

"It's nicer over there," Fred suggested gently, "than downtown."

"I still wish he'd let me come down."

She was beginning to feel very sad. Fred reached over and touched her shoulder. "Come on, Sarah Bernhardt," he said, "don't cry in your beer."

"Let's go dance somewhere."

"You're going home."

"This early?"

"You, my dear, are drunk."

"Hell," she said softly.

Even so, she was glad of his hand on her arm as they walked out. She held herself very stiff and proper and took one step at a time, not too slowly, but very carefully. The attendant at the parking lot was asleep in his lighted shack that looked for all the world like a phone booth.

"Wait." Fred tiptoed over and lifted his keys off the hooked board.

She was conscious that she was swaying very slightly when he came back. "Let the poor bastard sleep," he said.

"I wouldn't have done that," she said. "When it's his job and all."

"That's because you're basically mean and cruel."

"No," she said, "it's because the gravel is hurting my shoes."

He chuckled and, slipping an arm around her waist, steadied her along.

As they turned out of the lot, she said, "Let's put the top down."

"This, young lady, is not a convertible."

"Oh," she said. "I forgot. I thought you had a convertible."

"You are drunk."

She leaned back against the seat. He reached over and pulled her along the slick surface until she sat next to him. He swung one arm over her shoulder and pulled her still tighter.

"I am, sort of," she said. "I always know I am when I start talking about my father."

"And what's so strange about that?"

"Because I hardly ever saw him," she said.

"And that's exactly why."

She sighed. "Things are so simple for you."

"Maybe," he said, "things are just simple. Period."

She stopped trying to think and settled down to watch the lights go swimming past the windshield. A splatter of red and green. Then black. Then faint yellow, and more red and green.

"There's a moon," he said; "want to go out to the lake and neck?"

She nodded. He did not answer, but she was conscious now that he drove faster.

"It's an old moon" she said.

"What did you expect, this time of month, this time of night?"

"I guess I don't know the date, or the time either."

"Well, mercy sakes," he mimicked, "my little drunken friend."

"I wish I had a drink right now."

"You don't need it."

"I bet you've got some right in the glove compartment."

"Bet I do too."

"If you only had ice."

"I'll put in a refrigerator just for you."

"I want a drink."

"In a while, if you're a good little girl I'll give you one."

She stopped listening then and gave herself up to the long swooping rolls of her desire. Fred talked on. She could hear him from a great distance. At first she had tried to listen, to understand him. That had been months ago. Then she realized she didn't have to. He talked, joked even, from the time he switched off the car engine until the instant of his shuddering climax. Then after a brief interval, he began again.

She rather liked it. It was like having the radio on. It was soothing.

She heard the silence, she let herself drift on waves of alcohol and pleasure.

"You have been a good little girl," he said finally. "And like a gentleman I'll get you a drink."

He leaned over across the front seat, got the pint and the two shot glasses.

"Doesn't even burn," Joan said.

"Old Forester."

"You did want to make it a special evening."

"Did I?"

"The roses, and the whole thing seemed kind of that way."

"Maybe," he said quietly, "when I get to see you these days it seems like a holiday."

If she had said something then, it would have been all right. It would have been the way it was before. She knew it and she tried to think what to say. But her liquor-fogged mind moved slowly, and the words formed slowly: I won't work evenings any more, if you don't want me to. And I would also like to get married.

She delayed too long. She found exactly the right words but didn't get to use them.

He was mocking, lightly, with a change of mood: "Of course I know the library couldn't run without you."

"I like to work," she said faintly; "it keeps the summer from being boring."

"Sure," he said.

"Just that you want to do something different sometimes, not for any reason."

"To keep the summer from being so boring."

"Oh quit," she said wearily, "quit."

Aurelie stirred in her big four-poster, opened her eyes and stared up at the lace canopy that glowed faintly in the little crack of light from the hall. She heard it again, a second car door. Of course. They would be coming home, one of her two girls.

She got up and went to the window, lifting the corner of the shade gently, and peeped out. She recognized Joan's stocky figure, and then the street light fell on Fred's heavy handsome head.

A nice looking man, she thought, automatically. And then a second thought crossed her mind.

But she went back to bed. After a few minutes, she heard the front door slam, and then Joan's uncertain feet on the stairs. She's drunk, Aurelie thought with considerable distaste.

She seemed to have reached the top of the stairs. Aurelie could hear her stop for breath, trying to decide which way her room was. A soft thud of something light dropping, and then the steps shuffled off across the bare wood. Another stop and shoes were kicked off; one knocked into the wall, and Aurelie jumped. A door opened, too hard, and smacked into the wainscoting.

Aurelie sighed and got up. Since the house was very hot, she did not bother putting on a robe. The feel of the nylon nightgown drifting between her legs was vaguely pleasant.

As she expected, there were shoes in the hall, and a chiffon scarf, and over by the stairs, a purse had been dropped. She sighed again. The door to Joan's room was open and the little night light was burning. She stepped inside, knowing that she needn't bother being particularly quiet. Joan was sprawled face down crosswise on the bed, her feet still touching the floor. She was fully dressed.

Aurelie sighed again. Joan was the sloppy child. No matter how tired or drunk Doris was, she always managed to hang her clothes in the closet, including the time she had come home from a party after an accident with a bottle and her left hand sliced almost off, with eighteen stitches and a great wad of bandages.

Aurelie bent over and began undoing the back zipper. Joan did not move. When the dress and bra were opened, Aurelie shook her shoulder firmly. "Get up," she said.

Joan stirred vaguely. Aurelie pulled her to a sitting position—not gently—and dragged the dress over her head. She shook her again. "Now finish up yourself."

Joan stumbled out of her clothes. Aurelie held out a pajama coat. Some telltale stains and a certain odor— Aurelie wondered why she had had nothing but daughters.

"Joan," she said, "listen to me now. Are you being careful?"

"Huh?"

"Are you being careful, you heard me."

"Sure," Joan said. "I'm being careful and Fred's being careful too."

Aurelie let her slip back, and Joan was asleep before she touched the pillow.

Aurelie hung up the dress and left, closing the door firmly. She stepped over the shoes and the scarf on the hall floor. But she stopped by the purse, picked it up, and emptied its contents out on the little hall table. She blew into it carefully to remove the last speck of powder. Then took it back to her room. After all, it had only been borrowed, she remembered. It belonged to her.

5

THE Sunday that followed was a particularly bad day. The first bit of light was just beginning to show when Aurelie came back from Joan's room, tossed the little purse to her dressing table, and went over to the window. She pulled aside the curtains, the embroidered organdy curtains that were her special delight, and opened the shade. The window was high and looked directly into the big camphor tree, so she could see nothing of the ground, just the leaves and the sky above.

The air was very still, and almost cool. The odors of night jasmine and sweet olive had gotten all mixed up. They hung heavy and thick like streaks in the still air, or like incense at a funeral. The sky overhead was the strange color that comes just before light, a faint green. There didn't seem to be any traffic moving, even over on the avenue. It was very quiet, only the steady gurgling of the little fountain in the front yard and one sleepy confused squaak from a mockingbird.

Aurelie heard a sound she did not like—the stealthy

shifting of furniture upstairs. The last time she had heard that . . . No, she told herself firmly, that would not happen again.

She wondered briefly if she should go investigate Herbert's doings. But the stairs seemed so steep. . . . She went back to bed.

She had just slipped off to sleep when she heard Doris come home: the slamming of doors and then Doris herself stumbling along, singing at the top of her voice.

Girls, she thought, all girls. At least the other three aren't home.

And she went to sleep. Soundly, this time, black and dreamless.

At seven o'clock her phone, the little ivory-colored one with its unlisted number, began to ring. She glared at it for a bit before answering.

She listened patiently, said, "Yes, of course," and hung up.

Doris popped her head around the door. She was dressed in the inevitable white shorts and shirt and tennis shoes. "Who's getting you up so early in the morning?"

Aurelie looked at her with a mixture of annoyance and interest. "Child," she asked, "when do you sleep?"

"Don't," Doris giggled.

Aurelie shook her head gently.

"Only young once, little mother," Doris mimicked. "Who called you?"

Aurelie sighed again. "Your sister."

"Which one?" Doris said with a smirk, "I've got quite a few."

"Celine."

"What's the little bastard got into this time?"

"Honestly, child, that is no way to talk at all. She is a perfectly nice girl. . . ."

"Okay. What happened to her?"

"She got into poison ivy."

"At Camp what-do-you-call-it?"

"Owahkishmewah. She has a bad case, in her ears and under her eyelids."

"Gee," Doris said with her bright white grin, "what fun for the little monster."

"They called because they wanted to check before sending her in to the hospital at Willis Point."

"My, my," Doris said cheerily, "she must be near crazy."

Aurelie closed her eyes and settled down against the pillows.

"Don't go to sleep," Doris said, "I've got more news for you."

Aurelie's large yellow-brown eyes slipped open again. "You must have a remarkable liver," she said quietly. "You were drunk last night."

"It's about Papa Herbert."

Aurelie sat up abruptly, remembering the sounds of moving furniture she had heard hours earlier. "What?"

"When Clara came in for breakfast, about ten minutes ago, she found him sitting out in the back yard."

He had been sitting very quietly in the far corner of the yard, where the high board fence was almost covered with fragrant panicles of the tiny-flowered star jasmine. He was sitting quietly on a little white-painted iron bench; he was smoking cigarettes and he was naked.

"Oh God," Aurelie said.

"Clara's got a robe on him now."

"Oh," Aurelie said. "Oh, oh, oh."

"Seems they're after him."

"Who?"

"The feather merchants."

"Again," Aurelie said. "Oh not again."

"I've been talking to him," Doris said, "and do you want to hear the whole story?"

"Again," Aurelie repeated wearily. "I ought to have gone up there last night."

"He says he can't come in because his rooms are full of the feather merchants, but luckily he was able to trick them and slip on out and leave them locked in up there."

"Oh dear," Aurelie said, "oh dear."

"As a matter of fact," Doris lifted one eyebrow, "they're locked in the bathroom, if you want to know where they are, and he's piled all the furniture in front of the bathroom door to keep them in."

Aurelie rolled over and picked up the phone. "Tell Clara to stay there and I'll call for them to come get him."

"Tell that nice handsome Dr. Paul hello for me," Doris said.

"Don't sound like a nymphomaniac."

"He is handsome, looks just the way a psychiatrist should look."

Aurelie made the call quickly. There was nothing to arrange. It had all happened before. When she was finished, Aurelie stared into the phone she still held in her hand. "That does it," she said softly. Doris started at the change of tone. The grin slipped off her face.

Aurelie continued. "This is the last time. When he comes out of the hospital this time, he does not come back here."

The surprise passed. Doris was grinning again. "Well, farewell Papa Herbert."

"Hand me the note pad, child." Aurelie wrote a quick line.

"What's that?"

"Cousin William. I must call him the very first thing Monday morning."

"Divorce?"

"My dear child," Aurelie said, "I have put up with a great many years of this—far more than I have ever done with any man."

"He's been around so long," Doris said, "I thought he was permanent or something."

"Child," Aurelie said, "go to the bathroom and get me three aspirins and a glass of water."

She swallowed them. "So many years . . ."

"He's the helpless type," Doris said, "brought out the mother in you."

"Go away," Aurelie said.

When she left, Aurelie got up and turned the key in her lock, made herself go back to bed, stretch out under the sheet and close her eyes, pretending, even to herself, that she was asleep.

Aurelie was still in bed, Doris had gone, and Joan wasn't awake when Dr. Paul and two orderlies came by and picked up Mr. Herbert. There was a little procession of them, the four of them, Indian-fashion, from the kitchen where Mr. Herbert had been waiting (he had been having a beer with Clara; he carried the glass carefully in his left hand; his right was busily giving a crisp parade salute), through the hall and out of the front door.

The two orderlies were unnecessary. It was just something the hospital insisted on sending. Mr. Herbert Norton went with them, meek as could be. After all, in his entire life he had never made a fuss, he was always such a perfect gentleman. And he even seemed rather glad to be leaving.

JUNE ground along. In its last weeks, the sun got hotter and the sky turned a pale blue. Tremendous domed thunderheads with black underbellies sailed over almost every afternoon, dropped their loads of water in drenching downpours. Cars caught in the worst of those rains simply pulled over and stopped and waited. There were almost no pedestrians out—there was no staying dry in that kind of rain. Drops ricocheted off pavements and soaked clothes under raincoats; streets flooded knee-deep in a few minutes. Most people simply stayed wherever they happened to be during the afternoons. After all, it never rained before noon or after four.

When the clouds moved off and the sun came out, the leaves and pavements and houses shone fiercely, almost as if they were washed in oil. The air itself glittered with the bright clear sharp odor of ozone, left briefly from the violent lightning barrage. In half an hour or so all the wet surfaces began to steam, and the air turned dense and heavy, like the air in a greenhouse. And in the gardens the paper plants and the ginger lilies and the crinums almost visibly unfolded their waxy flowers.

The house on Coliseum Street drowsed behind its closed shutters (to keep out the rain) and its permanently opened windows. (Its high ceilings and echoing halls and leaky windows made it impossible to air-condition.) Aurelie got out her summer rugs of woven straw and her cotton slip covers. And she brought in her ferns and her potted violets.

"Place not only looks like a funeral parlor," Doris said, "it smells like one."

"A thankless child," Aurelie said and went about her work. When she was done and the house was really ready for summer, she packed her suitcase and went off to visit her cousins in Tennessee.

As she stood waiting for the taxi that would take her to the train, she said with a kind of wistfulness, "I went to Europe in the summers, before I had so many children to support."

Joan and Doris, who had to attend the ritual of seeing Aurelie off each year, stood on the porch too.

"Gee, that's tough," Doris said.

"Wait till your old age," Joan said, "and we have to support you."

"That," Aurelie said dryly, "is something I can wait for without any great impatience."

"Have a good time and give everybody our love."

"Be careful with the house," Aurelie said. "If there should be a real storm, don't forget to close the windows, and if the water comes through, mop it up right away."

The taxi arrived. Aurelie signaled to it.

"It'll probably be hit by lightning," Doris said, "with all those rods sitting up on the roof, attracting it."

"I will thank you," Aurelie said with dignity, "not to think evil."

"Yes ma'am," Doris grinned.

"And Clara will be in every day. . . ."

"Like last year," Joan said.

"And the year before," Doris said.

"And the one before that."

"Well," Aurelie said, "keep out of trouble when I'm gone."

"We'll think about you," Joan said, "up in those nice cool hills."

"With those nice yellow jacks," Doris added.

The driver had taken the suitcase.

"I'm jealous of anyone who can travel so light," Joan said.

"Comes of lots of practice," Doris said, "before she had children."

They walked down to the cab and Aurelie kissed them both good bye. "Keep out of trouble and be good."

Doris slammed the door with a flourish and the cab moved off along Coliseum Street. They watched until it turned at the corner.

Doris scratched a fast rising lump on her thigh. "Another damn mosquito."

"Let's go in."

"Well, old duck," Doris flashed her quick grin, "our four weeks of freedom has begun."

"I'll kind of miss her," Joan admitted.

"Jesus," Doris said. "Don't tell me you mean that?"

"I do, kind of."

"You're getting old, old duck. I can remember when you couldn't wait."

"I know."

"Would have thought better of you," Doris said.

"What are you going to do?"

"Haven't got a date until six o'clock."

"Don't you ever get tired?" Joan asked wistfully.

"Sometimes." Briefly, for a few seconds, Doris's handsome tanned face was serious. The crispness, the gayness slipped away; her face in repose was infinitely sad.

Joan had seen her like this before, not often, not more than once or twice a year, and never for long.

"The easiest way to get over being tired," Doris said seriously, "is just keep going."

"I wish I could."

"There's time enough for resting," Doris said. "Afterwards."

A flicker of something in the dark, heavily lashed eyes reminded Joan that her little sister had been death-haunted all through her childhood.

She's afraid, Joan thought, but she can swagger her way out of it.

Doris changed. The bright hard grin came back. She shrugged, "To hell with the whole business."

"Well," Joan said, "what are you going to do right now?"

"Me?" Doris said, "I'm going right straight up to Aurelie's bedroom and I'm going to lie right down on her bed, right on that precious spread, and I'm going to smoke cigarettes until the whole room stinks. Ain't that wicked?"

Without Aurelie the house seemed empty. Joan had never realized how much she had filled it.

Because she felt vaguely lonely and upset, Joan went to the kitchen and—in spite of Clara's threats—got out the recipe for angel food cake.

It failed. While Clara chuckled delightedly, she dumped it into the garbage can, stalked out of the yard. She caught the St. Charles car and rode around the belt three times before she felt like coming home.

5

TWO days after Aurelie left, on a Wednesday morning, Joan walked through the campus gate, headed for her music class. She was thinking about nothing in particular, but she just happened to raise her eyes. She stopped so short that she nearly stumbled.

Michael Kern was leaning on his elbows at a screenless window on the second floor, grinning down at her.

"For heaven's sake!"

"Wait a minute." He disappeared.

She wondered if she should stay right where she was. That didn't seem right, standing in the same spot, as if she were glued there. So she moved over to the steps and leaned, as casually as she could, on the railing. A minute or so passed and she wondered if she had misunderstood. She would look silly. . . . Maybe she just ought to go on. . . .

Then he came pounding down the steps. "Met some people and had to say hello."

She smiled, while having the strange feeling that

99

came to her when she heard about people in a world she didn't know. It felt sort of like being dead, she had decided once.

He was wearing a short-sleeved white shirt, and because it was early in the day the starched collar still stuck up crisply and the sleeves still kept their little peaks.

"You look mighty happy," she said.

"You know this is the first morning you looked up."

"The what?"

"You come by every morning."

"Sure I do," she said. "Of course I do."

"I've been seeing you pass every morning."

A little jolt, it wasn't fear, but it wasn't quite pleasant either. "I guess I just never looked up before."

"You go right straight on ahead. . . . Don't you ever look around or see who's passing?"

"I'm usually late in the mornings."

"Full of business."

"No," she said, "not particularly, there's just nothing to do around here in summer."

"The fun people are gone, huh?"

"Sort of."

"Why don't you go?"

"Can't afford the places I want."

"Yes," he said, "it always comes back to that."

She could feel the rough surface of the concrete pressing through her thin dress. She stood up.

"What's the hurry?"

"Just wanted to stand up."

"What's your class?"

"You wouldn't be interested."

He grinned. His side teeth were peppered with little gold fillings. "That's true."

"I've got just five minutes to get all the way over to Crampton Hall."

"I tell you what," he said, "I'll dismiss my class if you'll cut yours."

A large redbird was building an out-of-season nest in the sprawling gnarled crape myrtle. The tree itself was just coming into bloom. The fat green buds were beginning to burst open into ruffled white flowers. Joan stared up at it.

"Do you know," he said, "your eyes are bright blue in the sun."

"What have we got to do so urgent?"

"I'll tell you," he said, "and you won't believe me."

"Maybe not."

"I've got an aunt," he said, "or maybe she's a great-aunt, and she lives in Montgomery and she has a library."

"A real library, a public library?"

"A one-room library. . . . You'd like her. Nice old gal. You should see her house, right up on top a hill looking out on some other pitched roofs and cupolas all the way down to the Alabama River. I used to wonder why they call it a river when it's nothing more than a yellow creek full of garbage. You know, sometimes you can smell it clear up to the house when the wind's right in summer."

Joan looked down from the redbird and over directly at him. She was pleased to notice that her hard stare made him shift his eyes to a farther building.

"Anyhow," after a very short almost imperceptible pause, "this old gal has a library, pardon me, a room that she calls a library because it's full of books. . . ."

"I got it," she giggled.

"The books were left by her husband who didn't read them either. But there's one thing in there that she's particular about and they're getting kind of moldy."

"Moldy?"

"And that's why she needs a set of new owls."

"Of what?"

"Owls, honey child. There are stuffed owls sitting on the tops of the bookcases, one to each side of the room."

"And the moths got them."

"Some other bugs too. So she wants me to find her four new stuffed owls."

"Don't ask me," Joan said, "I wouldn't know where to tell you to go."

"I found one place. I think. It's hard as if I was looking for dope or something illegal."

"I don't think it *is* legal to shoot an owl."

"What's so particular about owls?"

"I don't know. I just thought I remembered seeing that somewhere."

"Oh God," he said, "now I've got to smuggle owls."

"But you found a place?"

He was staring out across the campus, scowling slightly. She noticed—again with surprise—that his eyes were dark and that they had ridiculously long curly lashes like a girl.

"That's where I want to go this morning. There's an old guy in Tangipahoa has some he'll sell me."

"This morning?"

"Miss Question-box. . . . Might be fun, who knows?"

"Okay," she said. "Let's go."

"Just so you don't get away," he grabbed her wrist and raced up the steps, "while I'm getting rid of my classes."

She was up the two flights almost before she knew it, and down a long dark hall, moving more rapidly than she had in months, conscious of the very tight pressure of his fingers. She wanted to say go slower, I can't keep up with you. But she was afraid he wouldn't hear or stop and people in the halls would turn around and wonder what was going on with him hauling her down the halls by one arm. So she kept up, skirts flying and hair falling in her face.

"Here," he said and turned abruptly into a side-office. He released her arm. "Look at the pretty books."

Obediently she turned and looked at the shelves of textbooks, conscious all the while that the three people in the office were staring at her very hard, all without seeming to look. Two were young men, the third a middle-aged woman typing at a small desk.

One of the men said very softly, "Been fishing?"

Michael did not answer him. She wondered if he glared or gave a sign. She could not turn.

"Mrs. Wright," Michael said very formally, "will you dismiss my classes today and tell them that I'm very sick."

"Sick with what?"

Joan could almost hear him grinning. "I don't know. Use your own imagination."

She gave a chuckle. "If the old man ever finds out about the rules that are broken around here every single day of the week!"

"He won't," Michael said. "Not when you do such a good job."

"Get on out of here and let some other people work."

"Yes, ma'am!"

Joan could hear the chatter begin the very moment they stepped into the hall.

THEY found the car and started off. "Aren't you afraid somebody will see you riding around like this with the top down? When you're supposed to be working, I mean."

"The old man," Michael gave his quick grin over his shoulder, "is at a seminar in the library. And that always runs two and a half hours."

Still, Joan noticed, he took the back way out of town, doubling and twisting along back streets through the narrow section of Carrollton. Finally he got on the old river road.

"God," he said, "I didn't think I could find it."

The road was very bad, and he had to drive slowly, cursing each pothole.

Joan could feel the hot sun burn her eyes. She began to wish she had brought sunglasses.

The pitted bumpy road turned into a new highway. "That does it, old girl," Michael said.

Then they were on the causeway, the straight narrow concrete strip that ran for twenty miles across the lake.

On each side the water glinted sharp points of light. Up in the sky, the inevitable thunderheads were poised.

"By the way," Joan yelled over the wind, "does your top go up at all?"

"Sometimes." Again that sharp animal grin. She decided that she liked it. She hadn't been sure before, but now she decided that she liked it. With a little sigh she settled herself down on the hot leather cushions, felt the wind whistling by her ears, ruffling out her hair. And she stopped thinking.

They swung off the causeway, and Michael slowed down. "God, it's hot."

"It doesn't seem to rain near as much here as it does in the city," she said. "It doesn't look like they've had a drop in weeks."

"Well," Michael said, "I don't know how long it's been but it's sure dusty right now." He rubbed the side of his face and wiped the palm across his shirt. "Want to stop for a beer?"

She nodded.

He turned down narrow winding roads, dirt paved, between rows of pine trees. "There's a place back in here," he said, "if I can find it."

"About half a mile more."

"You know it?"

"I used to come over here in the summers," she said, "when my father was here."

"Have I got the right road?"

"I think so."

It was a small bar with a corrugated iron roof and a Jax beer sign blinking in each window. In front was a parking lot of hard, swept white sand, studded with pine trees. The trunks of the trees were neatly whitewashed waist-high; up in their branches were strings of colored lights, and in one of them there was a loudspeaker from the jukebox inside.

Behind the building was another parking lot. The same white sand, only here the pine needles had been allowed to accumulate, and the trees grew closer together. There were no lights and there was just the soft muted leftover sound of the jukebox—she remembered that.

It had been a favorite spot for high-school kids. She wondered if it still was. . . .

The place was empty now, of course, with just one out-of-state license pulled up in front. But maybe at night it still was as crowded as it had been the times she'd come here. It had been jammed then; you'd have to hunt for a spot among all the other dark cars parked in the back lot.

It was funny, she thought, how little you remembered of those times, though they were so important then. And how the things you did remember were the unpleasant ones.

Like the time her corsage had gotten loose and the pin stabbed into her shoulder, drawing blood. And she had not been able to get the boy to understand, and she had been so embarrassed, drawing herself out of his arms and fumbling in her bag for a handkerchief to stop the blood.

And she remembered other things: the smell of bad grease from the chicken frying in the bar, the urine smell of the ladies' room that wasn't really a ladies' room, just a painted privy. The sour vinegar smell of the mustard on the sandwiches they always ordered and never wanted and never ate. The whispers from the other cars parked a couple of feet away. The feel of sweat-soaked shirts, sticky with starch, and skins that were hot and burning to the touch. And the smells inside the car: of upholstery and gasoline and after-shave and the heavy musky odor of sex.

She remembered pain too, fingers that were clumsy and hurt and bodies that were awkward and stiff. And the terrible feel of frustration coloring everything. Those evenings that were more pain and uncertainty than anything else, but desperately longed for and pursued.

Michael parked directly in front of the building. He did not ask her if she wanted to stay in the car, even though there were two drowsy carhops leaning against the side of the building. They went inside. "Would you like some lunch?"

"Too early for me."

The beer was cold, and the glasses heavy and frosty. She remembered those glasses, though back in the parking lot the frost had melted long before they reached the little tray on the side of the car window.

"Another?"

She jumped. She hadn't realized she'd drunk it so fast. "Yes," she said, "I would."

He laughed. "You've got more moods than anybody. The first time I took you out you sulked and hardly said anything."

"I did?" She could remember that evening. "You were something of a creep."

"And now you look like you're having a real fine time."

"I like it over here."

"Where'd you live?"

"My father had a place on the Tickfaw, and I used to stay with him in the summers."

"Still have it?"

"It was sold when he died."

"Oh," he said. "Well, drink up and let's go find the owls."

As they walked to the car she said, "My father was a remarkable man."

He winked to soften the words. "Doris always said that sooner or later you always started talking about him."

To hell with Doris, she thought. Aloud she said: "He really was. Anybody will tell you that."

"Except your mother."

"She thought he was dull." They got in the car. "She thought he was quiet and dull. Like me."

There was that wink again. "You're not quiet," he said.

He had a pencil-drawn map in his pocket and he began to follow it. They turned along a series of rutted sand roads and bounced slowly along between crumbling fences, undermined by honeysuckle and yellow jasmine. Under the scorching sun the perfume rose in heavy waves.

"There it is," Michael said.

It was a low house, with a porch on all four sides, a wire fence all around and chickens running loose inside the yard.

"I'll wait," she said.

He was gone a long time. The sun got unbearably hot. She left the car and walked over to the shade. She made herself comfortable, leaning against the rough bark of a big oak. Little lizards rustled up and down around her shoulders, but she did not move. She glanced at her watch, wondering what she would be doing if she were back at school.

After a few minutes a couple of rice birds began to fight in the top of the tree and she leaned her head back to watch them. All around was the close, heavy smell of mud baking brick-hard in the sun.

Michael came back, finally, carrying two stuffed owls. An elderly man followed, carrying one more. They put them in the trunk, after first wrapping them carefully in newspaper. Joan wandered over, scuffing her sandals in the loose dust of the road.

"Only got three," Michael said to her without turning around, "but Aunt Lucy will have to be content with a lopsided library."

They finished putting the owls away and slammed down the lid. "Thank you, sir," Michael said to the old man.

"Good evening," Joan said.

The old man blinked his pale blue eyes rapidly.

"You don't remember me," she said, "but I remember you."

"You was smaller," he said accusingly, "last time I seen you."

"I was younger."

"Anthony Mitchell's girl."

She grinned. "Remember how we used to live just a way over there?"

He rubbed the corner of his nose. "Place belongs to some people named Voorhies these days. Been sold twice."

"I heard about that," she said.

"Changed hands lots of times," he said, "not many people want that kind of place nowadays."

Michael was standing listening, looking puzzled. Joan turned to him. "It was a real big place," she said, "with a boathouse on the bayou and an artificial waterfall in the front lawn."

The old man laughed softly. "Cutting grass all the time, two boys, never did seem to get caught up."

"It was fun in the summers," she said.

"They never did catch him," the old man chuckled and turned back into the house. "Never did."

"No," Joan said to the bent crooked old back, "he just died."

"Let's go," Michael said. And when they started off, he asked: "Who didn't get him?"

"The federal tax people."

"I had heard about that," he said, "but I forgot."

"From Doris?"

"To hell with Doris."

"I don't want lunch," she said, "but I would like another beer."

"Soon as I can find my way out of these damn roads."

They found a bar (a new one this time; she did not remember ever seeing it before, and she liked it better because she did not). This time she waited. He came back with a dozen cold cans dripping in two paper cartons. "I didn't think you'd mind," he said, "but I thought we'd drive on up a little farther. That old guy back there told me about another owl that I could buy."

"Sure," she said. "You drive and give me the opener. . . . Where is this place?"

"Leesville road, but a little off it."

"Sure thing," she said. "I don't have to be back any special time. Even Aurelie isn't home."

She settled down against the cracked leather seat and watched the bright sky and thought a little more about an idea that had occurred to her. It had appeared quietly, about half an hour before, while she had been leaning on the big oak tree. She felt the car turn off the hard-surfaced road, but she didn't bother looking around.

"Open me another can, old girl," he said.

She did, scarcely noticing. The dust was heavy in the air now, and she sneezed.

"These fucking roads," he said softly under his breath.

She kept perfectly still, letting the idea drift in and out of her mind, playing with it, turning it round and about with a touch of her mental fingers, imagining it a wind harp.

She lost track of time. It must have been quite awhile, because her throat was dry and nasty tasting from the dust. (She had forgotten about the beer. Michael had not. There were five empty cans lined up on the top of the dash.) The car braked to a stop. She saw Michael hunched over the wheel, too furious to curse. She sat up. They were at the end of a rutted weed-filled road that looked as if it hadn't been traveled in months. Directly ahead of them was the house, a small peaked-roof house, its windows boarded with broken planks, its door yanked off so that a small black hole showed on the front. It was abandoned, that was for sure, and it had been that way for some time, because the fast impatient creepers had already inched up the side of the house and pushed through the boards of the porch.

"Things go to pieces so quick around here," she said, as if that would explain.

"For God's sake . . . the old bastard had it all wrong."

"Maybe he didn't know. Or maybe he thought it was funny."

"Oh God."

"Have the rest of the beer," she said, "and stop fretting. We just go back the way we came."

He managed a grin. "Might as well."

"Bring the can and we'll go see what's inside."

There was nothing inside, except a great many lizards that fled as they approached, and gigantic sleepy roaches, shiny black in the light.

The empty house and the soft gloom was solemn, and a little frightening too. It was all the childhood tales of haunted houses. Vague horrors looked out from the bare, paint-streaked walls. They stood a little closer together, even when they stood in the sun of the weed-grown yard.

"What do we do now?"

It wasn't so much a question as an invitation. And her own idea that had been hovering about her eyes. . . .

She laughed aloud, a delighted tinkle, which surprised even herself. She had never heard that sound before.

"What's so funny?"

"If you're the sort of guy I think you are, you've got a blanket rolled up nice and neat in that trunk."

"I always carry a blanket," he said.

"And back up on the side there," she pointed, "there's a stand of lovely pines. And nothing grows under pines, no brambles, no bushes. Just needles, all soft. We could take a rest up there before we go on back."

He stared at her for a minute. "I'll be damned."

"Unless you'd rather go right back."

"No," he said, "I just wanted to be sure I had it all straight."

He got the blanket. In the pines it was soft and clear. And fragrant smelling under the quiet hot day. The light was gentler too—not the purple light of the old closed house, but the soft filtered light of a bedroom with shades drawn.

They must have slept because when they next noticed, the locusts had started to signal from the tallest trees. And there was a raging hunger in their stomachs that told them plainly that they had not had lunch.

Joan brushed back her dress and ran a quick comb through her hair. Michael folded the blanket and they walked back to the car, silently. The shadow of the house stretched across the weed-choked yard now and reached right to the parked convertible, flowing over it like water. And when they got in, Joan noticed that the leather was almost cool to her hand.

THE next morning she changed her route to school. Almost without thinking, she shifted her path. It meant an extra-block walk in the summer sun, but it also meant that she need not pass that one particular building. It seemed to her the only polite thing to do.

She did not see him on the campus. And he did not call. She had not expected that he would. It hadn't been that important.

And that was June.

II. END OF THE SUMMER

WITH the first sign she told herself severely, Don't be silly.

So she forgot it for another four weeks. And then, still unbelieving, for another three.

One morning, one still clear morning in early September, she woke up. Suddenly. It was quite early. Her clock had stopped but she could tell by the light that it couldn't be much more than five o'clock. She lay looking at the papered ceiling, crisscrossed with little cracks and stained with faint beige mold. And the truth that she had forgotten passed slowly in front of her mind.

Fred's been careful, and I've been careful. Except for once. Just once. How silly.

She did not feel alarmed. She was merely curious.

This is how you tell, she thought. It's a feeling after all. Heavy and lazy and smug and full. And how big was the child, she wondered. It would look something like a shrimp, or a piece of seaweed.

She didn't feel tired, or sick. Just content.

God, she thought, I must be the motherly type after all.

She twisted her mouth up wryly. Turned over, and went back to sleep.

When she woke again, the feeling of well-being was gone. She felt very busy. She was not alarmed. There were certain things to be done and she was all impatient to get to them.

She had a quick shower and dressed with more speed and decision than usual. She made up carefully and put on lipstick with a brush, the way she almost never did. When she was finished, she looked up Michael Kern in the phone book. He was listed. She was vaguely surprised. But of course there was no reason why he shouldn't be.

She took a straight chair from its position against the wall and brought it over, so that she wouldn't muss the fresh starch of her cotton skirt. Sitting primly and straight, she dialed the number.

He answered almost at once. She recognized his voice, muffled and angry.

"I woke you up," she said, "I'm sorry."

"Who the hell is this?"

"Joan," she said, "Joan Mitchell."

A pause and a yawn. "Hi, honey bunch."

"Can you get dressed? I've got to see you."

"Oh God," he groaned softly, "not now."

"Yes, now," she said gently, "I think it had better be right now."

"I've got to shave and I was up late."

"I won't come up," she said, formally, "if you're worrying about that."

"Nine o'clock on a Saturday morning—God!"

"Do you know the drugstore right on the corner of Carrollton? It can't be more than three or four blocks away from you."

"Sure," he said flatly, "I know it."

"It'll take me half an hour to get there," she said, "on the streetcar."

"I've got to shave."

"That's plenty of time."

"Oh God."

"I wouldn't if it wasn't important." She hung up then, before he should say more.

She recombed her hair, shook a quick dash of cologne on her skin. And left.

WHEN she got off the streetcar she opened her umbrella: she had a block to walk in the sun. The silk
protection felt safe and tight. The heat filtered through
the pale beige and turned to a soft glow around her
shoulders. I should wear more beige, she thought, it's
a good color for me. A beige silk would be nice. And
what was the name of that. . . . Tussah silk, that
would be it. It would be expensive, but it would be so
flattering with a soft skirt and just a hint of petticoat
underneath.

In the drugstore the usual clutter of shelves and
counters and paper pennants overhead. And an odor
that was a mixture of camphor and disinfectant and
toasting bread. The usual kids, aimless, school-less,
perched on the stools at the fountain. Pimply kids,
heads close together, giggling.

She glanced down the line of tables. Michael was not
there. So she selected one in the middle and sat down
carefully. "Coke," she ordered; then, "No, iced tea."

The shiny black table top was almost hidden by doodles: JBF l SWR and a phone number UP6784 and vague geometrical designs. She sugared her tea carefully and asked for extra pieces of lemon and ignored the waitress's grimace. She was sipping away with methodical slowness when Michael Kern arrived.

"I didn't really expect you to be on time," she said. He looked fresh and starched; his hair was very wet and showed the marks of the comb.

"Mysterious phone call, mysterious lady. What else could I do?"

He was in better humor, she thought; but then nobody felt good when they had been yanked out of bed, not for the first minute. His face looked pink and freshly shaved.

"You use a straight razor," she said almost accusingly.

"I use a Gillette," he corrected.

"I meant not an electric."

He shook his head, looking puzzled.

"You see," she plunged along, "I could tell. You've cut yourself."

He lifted a hand to his chin.

"No," she said, "way back on your cheek. By your ear."

He touched gently. The blood had dried.

"It's nothing," she said hastily.

His coffee came and he winked at her over the cup rim. "Now what's going on, mysterious lady?"

She looked down the straws into the lemon-cloudy tea. She felt that this wasn't the way to go about it.

"I'm pregnant," she said.

She did not look up for a couple of seconds. His face when she saw it was completely expressionless. She went back to her tea, sipping slowly. I've told him, she thought, now he has to say something.

"Are you sure?"

"Yes."

"And how are you sure it's me?"

"Because it's the only time nobody was careful."

Now he was staring at the milky coffee in the purplish-blue plastic cup. "Good God," he said slowly, "just once."

"We forgot to be careful."

"I thought you would be."

She smiled with one corner of her mouth. "I didn't expect anything that day, you remember, and it isn't the sort of stuff you carry in your purse to school."

Now that they had started talking about it, she felt better. There was no longer the problem of beginning. For better or worse, they had started. There was nothing to do but follow along.

"It's not anybody else, with me for the fall guy?"

"I keep telling you," she said patiently. "And the timing is right."

"God, why didn't you think about that then?"

"I didn't, though," she said. "Nobody ever does. Then. Only after."

Seaweed child, she thought, floating about, having iced tea at a Walgreen Drug Store with yellow and red paper advertisements waving overhead. . . . She looked up and read them off silently: Milk of Magnesia, Bayer Aspirin, Creo Mulsin for Colds.

"You were smiling," he said. "For God's sake why?"

"It's such a strange place to be talking about this sort of thing."

"Worse than under some pines?"

"No," she said quietly, "I guess every place is strange."

The waitress was looking and he ordered another cup of coffee. "What do we do?"

She looked over the store, out at the lazy half-empty midmorning store. "I was asking you that."

He started to run his hand through his hair, then remembered it had been freshly combed, and lit a cigarette instead. "Well," he said, "if you say I'm the guy for this, I guess I am." And he added bitterly, "Even if I'm not, nobody would ever believe it."

"You are," she insisted quietly.

"You want to get married? Girls always want to get married."

"I don't know," she said, "I hadn't thought about it."

Her answer seemed to confuse him. He was quiet for a moment. But she couldn't tell from his face what he was thinking.

"Or," he said, "you could go away and have it. Somewhere."

Floating child, she thought, do you feel the pull of the moon, do you feel tides? Do you feel the sway of a walk down the hard pavements?

"Or," he said, slowly, "you could get rid of it."

"Yes," she said, "I know I could."

Some little kids were standing at the ice-cream counter. They were arguing over the flavor of the cone they were going to share. Joan watched them in silence. One yelled for chocolate, her sister for coffee. They finally settled for strawberry.

Michael seemed to feel that he should say something. Joan felt him shifting in his hard seat.

"Look," he said finally, "don't get me wrong, or anything like that."

"Oh no," she said hastily and politely.

"Let me finish. . . . I'm not running out on you, or anything like that. If you want to get married, God, we'll get married."

"Yes," she said slowly, "we could do that."

He shook his head. "I don't know," he said, "but it seems to me like you're awfully calm. For this. I thought gals got upset."

"I'm not upset," she said, "I just don't know what to do."

"Damn'dest thing. . . ."

"It never happened to me before."

"Me neither," he said with a sour smile.

She just nodded.

"We can get married, you know. Maybe it wouldn't be too bad."

"Do you know how big it is now?" she asked abruptly.

"What?"

"The child."

"No," he said, "it can't be very big."

"No."

"Did you hear what I told you?"

"Yes," she said, "let's get out of here."

As he paid the bill, she said: "I'll go now. I'll let you know in a couple of days."

"Okay."

She touched his shoulder, gently, casually. Just the way you would tell a small boy good bye. And on her way out she stopped and bought a pack of chewing gum.

AURELIE was gardening. Not that she knew one plant from the other. But her yearly trip to the mountains of Tennessee gave her a vaguely guilty feeling. Her cousins gardened. And it was lovely. They wore wide hats and puttered around the shady part of the gardens, by the rhododendrons. And every hour or so a white-coated butler brought them glasses of iced tea, sweetened with rum or bourbon, and they rested on the little benches and looked out across the valley to the nearest ridges of the Smokies.

Aurelie was jealous. It was part of a lady's life, this gardening; and it was a part she was missing. When she got home she had promptly ordered a set of copper gardening tools from Hammacher Schlemmer. They arrived a week later and the box, unopened, had been lying on the top of the refrigerator in the kitchen.

This morning, passing it, she knew she could no longer put off. So she got on her gardening outfit—white shirt and full-skirted denim jumper. It smelled faintly musty because it had not been used since last year—but the air would soon take care of that.

She looked over the garden. With the shiny new tools in her hand, she surveyed the handkerchief-sized back yard, the narrow strips on each side of the house, wide enough only for a brick walk and ribbon-sized edging beds. She selected the east side finally, because it was shady. Settling herself on her little gardening stool, and giving her hair one final clean-handed pat, she began grubbing around the roots of the blue hydrangeas and the violets.

Joan came back from the drugstore, walking slowly in the noon sun. Her starched dress was beginning to wilt and there were dark splotches of perspiration across her back. Her petticoat stuck to her legs and she yanked at it as she entered the house. She stopped in the kitchen, grunting good morning to Clara. She found an orange and ate it, sucking it through a hole in the skin with loud noises.

Clara kept silent until she was almost finished. Then she said: "You mother hear you, and she go right through the roof."

"I'm a grown woman," she said, "not a child."

Clara shrugged patiently, "Okay, woman-grown."

Joan finished and tossed the skin into the garbage pail. "Where is my mother?"

Clara grinned secretly out the kitchen window. "Gardening."

"Where?"

"Outside. Where else you find mud?"

Joan slammed the screen door behind her. She heard the steady chink chink of the trowel and followed it to the east side of the house. Aurelie did not look up. She kept right on jabbing the trowel into the wet earth.

"Such pretty tools," Joan said finally, "seems a shame to get them dirty."

"Just hold them under the faucet," Aurelie said in time with her jabs, "and they will be good as new."

"As a matter of fact," Joan said, "they'd look kind of pretty sitting alongside a window garden. You know— herbs or something like that."

"An herb garden." Aurelie studied her own right hand, which kept moving up and down of its own accord. "I've never thought of that."

"You just sliced up a worm."

Aurelie glanced down. "Nasty things."

"I've got to talk to you," Joan said.

"Won't it wait until lunch?"

"No," Joan said.

"Oh child of my heart, everything will wait a few hours."

"I've got to do something," Joan said, "and I don't know what to do."

"Nonsense," Aurelie said, "young people always know what to do."

"There are a couple of things I could do," Joan said, "and I want to know which one."

"There's another worm," Aurelie said, "dear me, the ground must be full of them."

"It's the violets," Joan said. "They're always around violets." She added: "I'm pregnant."

The little trowel stopped jabbing. Aurelie looked up. "Are you saying you've eloped?"

"No," Joan said. A hummingbird swooped into the narrow passage, was frightened by their figures, and swooped out frantically.

"You're not secretly married?"

"No."

Aurelie got off her canvas stool, collected her tools, and carried everything into the back yard. She placed the stool neatly in a corner of the kitchen porch, then rinsed the one muddy trowel under the garden faucet. She put the tools carefully away in their rack on the wall, next to the barometer. She took off her gloves and hung them over the railing.

She started inside, then abruptly turned back and wiped dry the one trowel, polishing it carefully on her skirt. She checked the other tools. They were clean; their copper winked and glistened in the morning sun.

"All right now," she said quietly.

Joan followed her inside, into the little room that served as a study. Aurelie closed the door, firmly. "Is it Fred?"

"No."

"I would prefer not to know then," Aurelie said.

"Poor Fred," Joan thought out loud, "if I told him,

he'd probably marry me right away on the chance that it might be his."

"There will be none of that," Aurelie said very firmly.

"No," Joan said, "I wasn't planning that."

Aurelie walked over to stare out of the window, even though the shutters were drawn tightly against the hot morning sun. "How long has it been?"

"Two months," Joan said, "nearer three, I guess."

Aurelie inspected the closed blinds carefully again. I can't tell from her back, Joan thought, what she's thinking or feeling. But at least there's no scene. I knew she wouldn't make a scene.

"If it's that long," Aurelie said to the window, "something's got to be done at once."

"Yes," Joan said. "I know that."

Aurelie did not seem to hear. "I'll call Ethel tonight. You can stop there. . . ."

Joan thought: she always says stop for stay.

"You haven't had a vacation," Aurelie turned around finally, "so you're going to spend a little time with your aunt."

"Yes," Joan said.

"It can be done easier at the Pass."

Joan leaned one shoulder against the wall. It's all decided for me, she thought, I knew it would be. "How big do you suppose it is?"

"I have no idea," Aurelie said coldly. "Why don't you go pack a suitcase for a week at the Pass?"

"Right now?"

"Tonight's train," Aurelie said, "or tomorrow's."

Joan shrugged. "Sure."

Aurelie said, "You won't go trying any homemade remedies, child."

"I know," Joan said, "I don't particularly want to kill myself."

"Thank God," Aurelie said dryly, "you have a small amount of common sense left."

Back in her room, and alone, Joan thought: it should have been more dramatic, somebody should have yelled. It's so casual, and easy.

Aurelie stopped by an hour later. "The evening train will be fine. Ethel will meet you."

"Thanks," Joan said. And then: "What will you tell Doris?"

Aurelie arranged her lips into a straight, patient line. "Why?"

"I just don't want her to know."

Aurelie kept looking at her. How much could she guess, Joan wondered. But she couldn't. She couldn't possibly guess.

Joan kept her face empty and calm. After a moment Aurelie said: "I don't see why Doris should be told anything."

"She'll find out."

"Oh honestly now," Aurelie said, "do try to be a little bit sensible. Even now, when it is rather late for that sort of thing."

"She'll find out," Joan insisted.

"*Mon Dieu*," Aurelie said. And left.

To her back and the closing door, Joan said again: "Thanks though. Thanks a lot."

She remembered the rest in a kind of daze. She felt curiously left out. Everyone else moved with such purpose. They all knew what they were doing and they didn't bother to tell her. Looking back, she saw that it reminded her of the school ballet when she had been perverse enough not to learn her steps. Then the stage was filled with people going about their business, whirling about. And she stood, one foot stepping on the other, nervous hands clasping and unclasping behind her back.

It was rather like that now. She did nothing. People moved about because of her, but not including her.

She didn't know what to do. At first it annoyed her and then she gave up and contented herself with following the hints others gave her. She found she was much happier that way, watching the plot unfold, like an observer.

She took the three o'clock train. At six she was emerging from the embrace of her great-aunt Ethel—tall, thin, gaunt in her old age, but still striking and with a startling resemblance to Aurelie. "My dear, how well you look," Ethel said.

"You don't change a bit," echoed Joan.

And in the car (the same 1929 Rolls she had bought

fifteen years ago) Ethel said the exact same thing to the
chauffeur that she had been saying for years: "Don't go
fast, Peter. We have nothing important to do."

How many times had he heard that? Joan wondered.
But he probably didn't even listen any more.

"It's been such a long time since you've come over,"
Ethel said. "It's been ages."

"I know," Joan said, following her lead obediently.
"I've missed the Pass."

"As soon as we knew you were coming," Ethel went
on, "I had to call up Roger and tell him you'd be here."

She had almost forgotten him—a tall thin man, who
was in the lumber business somewhere along the coast.

"And of course," Ethel went on, "the moment he
heard he just *begged* me to have you save him the Yacht
Club Dance. He's been perishing for a glimpse of you."

"Oh yes," Joan said vaguely.

"So he'll pick you up around nine."

"Tonight?"

"Dear, dear, today is *Saturday*."

Joan hedged nervously. "I am sort of tired, though,
and I've got a slight headache and I really thought I
would just curl up early tonight."

Ethel's eyes flashed a warning at her. She had made
a mistake. "Oh really, dear, you can't miss the most important thing of the summer. And I don't think it will
hurt your cold. At least I hope not."

So that was it, Joan thought. She was going to be in-
disposed for a few days with a cold. . . . It would take

only a few days, of course. She kept thinking of it as more of a problem than it really was.

"I'm just dying to go," she lied aloud, "and I don't suppose it could do any harm."

"As long as you don't get chilled."

And there it is, Joan thought, all fixed for me.

"I do like to see the young people have fun," Ethel said. "It reminds me of my youth. You wouldn't believe it, you youngsters, but I was nineteen once too."

"You're not old," Joan said, properly.

"Oh yes I am," Ethel said piously, "but I love to see young people have fun. I really do, deep down in my heart I do."

Joan got in very late that night. As she climbed the stairs to her room she noticed that her legs ached. And they never had before. Her back bothered her too, as if she had been carrying something heavy and had almost strained it.

And why did she feel that way, she wondered, groggily. There wouldn't be any weight to the child. Not yet. And there wouldn't ever be.

She was sleeping heavily, snoring gently with her mouth half open, when there was a knock on the door. "Go away," she muttered.

Her aunt came into the room and shook her shoulder.

She had to open her eyes. The curtains were still drawn and the room was dim. "What time is it?" she asked stupidly.

"Almost seven," Ethel said. She was making it sound like a picnic. The undertones said so clearly: if you don't hurry you'll miss all the fun.

"I haven't had any sleep," Joan said.

"You can rest later, dear."

Joan blinked her eyes slowly. Her aunt was walking around the room, busily, opening curtains.

"Your clothes are all ready. Rise and shine!"

Joan stumbled out of bed, falling over her own feet, stretching endlessly as her joints snapped.

"Oh dear," Ethel said. "I do hope you're not going to be arthritic. Those joints sound suspicious to me." She handed Joan her clothes, keeping up a line of patter as she did. "We don't want to keep them waiting. They've been so very nice to do things on short notice."

Who? Joan thought. For what?

Then she remembered and there was a little tremor like fear in her stomach. "But today's Sunday," she said, "I didn't think it would be Sunday."

"One day's as good as another," Ethel said cheerily, handing her a pair of stockings.

"No," Joan said, "I'm not going to wear stockings and heels." She got a pair of sandals from the closet herself.

There was a little wicker basket, like a purse, standing on the dressing table. Joan did not remember seeing it before.

"You can put a few things in here," Ethel said. "Few what?"

"Mercy, child," Ethel said, "brush your hair."

I'm not a child, Joan thought fiercely, so stop calling me one. I'm a woman and I'm carrying another generation inside of me. A tiny point of life, a floating point of life.

But she said nothing. And Ethel did not seem to notice her rigid defensive stance as she went right on calmly packing the little wicker case. It was too full. She had to empty it and start over. Joan stared at her as she filled the bag (more carefully this time) with a bedjacket Joan had never seen before—she herself didn't own one—a bottle of make-up, a box of powder, and two lipsticks. She added a small bottle of cologne, unopened. "L'Heure Bleu," she said, "how I love that myself. Even an old woman like me, I use it all the time."

Where did they come from, Joan thought: jacket and perfume. Does she have a special supply for relatives in trouble?

Ethel closed the basket. "Ready?"

It was on the tip of Joan's tongue to say no, but instead she nodded her head. Things seemed more like a play than ever; nothing was going to happen; nothing was real.

They went down the long halls and the stairway, steep and black and empty. Joan was surprised to see how dark the center of the house was. She had never noticed it before; there had always been lights on before—not too many, just a few well-placed bulbs. Discreet would be the word.

That thought made her chuckle silently. Ethel really was the soul of discretion. Like having all this arranged early on a Sunday when none of the house staff came on duty until noon.

The car was parked outside, in the drive, where it always was. Joan giggled again silently when she saw her aunt slip behind the wheel. Ever, ever so discreet.

Her aunt drove rapidly with a kind of grim concentration. They turned away from the Gulf and headed north. The roads were empty at this hour and Ethel drove very fast.

I wouldn't have guessed it, Joan thought. I wouldn't have thought she'd tear along. . . . And why does she keep Peter to drive for her?

The seat was hard. Joan shifted uneasily. Ethel noticed that.

"It isn't very comfortable, is it, child?" She smiled a grim winter smile without taking her eyes off the road. She dodged a large grey rabbit that crouched in the right lane. "Only the chauffeur and the footmen were supposed to sit up here."

"Oh," Joan said.

They hit a particularly large rut. Joan caught herself with both hands against the dashboard. Ethel slowed down slightly. "Well," she said, apologizing to no one in particular, "there are some crossroads coming soon and somebody might just be out."

It was a foggy morning, warm and close. There were black streaks of mosquitoes too and lots of night bugs were still out: they spattered against the windshield with popping sounds like tiny rocks.

It did not occur to Joan to ask questions. Not until she was tucked into the high hospital bed with the harsh sheets scratching her body and the unfamiliar bedjacket over her shoulders. It seemed kind of silly then to say to her aunt who was just leaving: how is it done? and, does it hurt? and, when will they do it?

It seemed so silly to ask that of her aunt whose thin voile-covered body stood patiently by the bed. She had just finished stacking a great pile of new magazines on the little table. Where had they come from? Joan wondered. She hadn't noticed them before.

"Now," her aunt said matter of factly, "I have to get back in time to have people for lunch. Did we forget anything?"

"No," Joan said. "This is just fine."

Why didn't she ask? Not even: how long?

But she didn't. And her aunt kissed her on the forehead and went out.

Joan stared at the wall for awhile and jumped guiltily when a cheery little nurse popped in the door demanding: "How are we doing here?"

"Fine," Joan said.

"Mustn't get blue," the little nurse said, "after all there's nothing to it, nothing to worry about."

"I wasn't worried."

"Mustn't just sit and stare, bad for the nerves and the disposition and it puts wrinkles in the pretty forehead."

The nurse giggled, proud of her own joke. "Look at the pile of lovely magazines."

You can have them, Joan started to say. But the nurse only picked up one and opened it at a random page and held it up close to her nose. Joan took it automatically. "That's better," the nurse chuckled. "That's a whole lot better."

Joan held the magazine, not reading, but turning a page now and then, in case somebody else should pass through the door. Once—after a few minutes—she laughed out loud. That was when she remembered that she had forgotten to tell Michael. She had forgotten completely.

And later, drifting off pleasantly enough, she thought of it again—forgot to tell him—and she giggled her way into unconsciousness.

IT was over then and done with.

Joan came back to her aunt's house at Pass Rigaud. The windows were open, and the same steady wind was blowing in from the Gulf and the same locusts were singing in the trees at the first sign of evening.

The same sound that there had been at another house, a deserted house. With the thick stifling odor of pines in the hot hot sun. . . .

She remembered that. She kept remembering that. And why do I do it, she thought, when it's over and finished with?

And there wasn't a breath of air that day. . . .

"I feel so tired," she told her aunt. "I feel so terribly tired."

"A rest will be fine for you," Ethel said. "Good pine air after that awful damp in New Orleans."

And she had the sleeping porch made up for Joan. Without asking her. Joan moved out there obediently.

"This will be wonderful for you," Ethel said. "In the

old days they used to say it was good for consumptives, too."

So Joan slept on the porch and heard the soughing of the pines all night, and woke to the sharp stifling smell of their needles when the morning sun grew hot on them.

"I'm cold out there," she complained after the first night. And she took two blankets and a quilt out with her the next time. She rolled herself up in them like a sleeping bag for warmth.

It seemed to her sometimes that the wind blew right through her, echoed right through her. And it was in those long quiet nights, looking up at the stars through the haze of the screen wire, that she became aware of her body's emptiness. She had always thought of herself as solid. A solid lump. Like a piece of mud or even a roast in the oven. But now she knew she wasn't. That she was just a tissue of skin stretched around a frame of bone. Like a canoe or a tent. She had seen wind or rocks break them up, and it bothered her to be stretched so fine and delicate.

She lay at night listening to the echoing emptiness inside her, caverns and echoing passages of bones, empty rooms and cages one after the other.

She did not go out. She turned down each subsequent invitation—tennis, a quick sail, a moonlight swim—with almost the same words: "I'm so tired. I haven't been feeling well."

Her aunt added an explanation for her when it was

necessary: "The summer flu—it is so hard to get over, you know."

Her face was thinner. Each morning darker circles under her eyes stared at her; and each morning resolutely she covered them with make-up.

"Dear child," her aunt said one morning at breakfast, "that particular stuff gives you an absolutely porcelain look. As if you might break."

"I might," she said, "I'm crispy and brittle."

"Honestly child, you've been ill, but there's no need to take on."

And so (she had a feeling her aunt arranged it, but she had never been able to figure out just how) she began gardening. Or rather she spent hours crouched in the sun, running the soft sandy dirt between her fingers.

Occasionally too she would take an old slaughter pole that she found stored up on the rafters over the garage and go down to the end of the pier and fish. The Gulf was very shallow and she would watch the big blue crabs scuttle by. She never caught any fish. Once she hooked an eel, but she snipped her line and let him go.

She didn't particularly care. It was the heat she wanted. The white sun pouring in through the straw of her hat, the white sun glaring up from the surface of the water beneath her.

It was only in the full sun that she felt warm and comfortable.

5

JOAN stayed on the coast longer than she had intended. The endless, unruffled hot days stretched along. The brilliant white summer color left the sky. The clouds were piled higher and more fiercely than ever and the hurricane season approached. She had no word from the house on Coliseum Street. Sometimes she got a strange feeling that it wasn't there at all.

Aurelie called occasionally, she knew. Because Ethel would say casually at dinner, "Your mother sends you her love." So she had telephoned. But Joan did not ask to speak to her, and Ethel did not suggest it.

Fred wrote her once or twice, short gossipy letters, that didn't sound like him at all. Joan wondered what Aurelie had told him.

She asked Ethel once: "What did Aurelie tell Fred?"

"Now, dear," Ethel said.

"I want to know."

The old eyes twinkled with something that was either maliciousness or amusement (Joan couldn't decide which). "She told him the truth, of course—that you were very tired and nervous and a bit overwrought."

"Oh," Joan said.

Again the unidentified gleam. "A common complaint of young females."

As Joan sat on the end of the pier with her pole a few minutes later she rehearsed her aunt's words. She knew then what they were planning to do. They were all going to pretend that it hadn't happened.

Her heart jumped around her chest crazily, like a bird fluttering. She wondered if she was going to faint.

They were going to pretend it hadn't happened, that nothing had happened. But it had. Of course it had.

They had to pretend. Always.

She studied the smooth yellow surface of her pole, running her index finger up and down along it. The fluttering stopped, and she felt steadier.

How strange, she told herself. It must have been the sun.

She did not realize she had spoken aloud until she saw an old man, who was fishing some dozen yards away, turn and stare at her.

A few days later, as she came into the house, she found her aunt waiting for her on the front porch.

Joan was drenched. One of the fierce quick afternoon thunderstorms had caught her. Her blouse was plastered to her, transparent as veiling, so that the outline of her bra showed. Her hair dripped behind her ears.

"It was a hard rain," Ethel said. "It seems to get harder each day."

"Yes," Joan said. She climbed the steps, stopping just outside the front door, and waited.

"You go right in and change." Ethel was wearing a purple print dress with little white ruching around the neck. An old woman's dress. "I've got a message for you, though."

"What?" Joan asked.

"Aurelie is coming in the morning."

"Oh," Joan said.

"Fred is driving her over."

"Oh," Joan said.

"I've always wanted to meet that young man," Ethel said. "After all, I really should meet my nephew-in-law at least once before the wedding."

Pretend that nothing has happened. . . . "Okay," Joan said. "I'll toss my stuff into the suitcase." She gave a quick bright smile that missed Ethel somehow and flashed on a window and a bit of shutter as she turned to go inside.

She had to stop a minute, dazzled as she was from the glare. And as she waited for her eyes to adjust, she shivered in her wet clothes, shivered in the cool dusky hall.

And that was how she went back to New Orleans, back to the house on Coliseum Street.

III. THE HOUSE
ON COLISEUM
STREET

THEY came back on a Saturday. On Sunday morning Doris banged into Joan's room. Joan had not gotten up; she was lying on her side, studying the shape of her hand against the sheets, studying the nails and the little half-moons at their base.

"Welcome home, old duck," Doris said cheerily.

Joan looked up. As she did, she realized that her eyes ached. Their lids were heavy and swollen. Have I been crying, she thought suddenly. Was I crying in my sleep?

She scrubbed at her eyes. "God, I sleep hard."

Doris dropped down on the foot of the bed. She was wearing a white nylon robe, a birthday present from Aurelie, and her hard tanned body showed clearly through the filmy gauze. Her short blond hair was flattened on one side, where she had slept, and her cheek still had the pink creases of the pillow. She looked rumpled and half awake, and the enormous collar of her robe was bunched up like ruffled feathers. She slapped at it once or twice, irritably.

"Trust Aurelie to pick something like this," she said. "This just isn't my style."

"Yes it is," Joan said. "You should have a bedroom all mirrors and gold sea shells. Venus rising and that sort of thing."

"I know," Doris grinned. "High-class whore house."

Joan sat up, feeling the familiar dizziness begin to sing in her ears. Then quite suddenly it stopped; her head was clear and empty.

Doris bounced on the foot of the bed, the filmy nylon fluttering over her body like clouds over rock. "So tell me what went on."

Sitting up, Joan did not have to open her eyes so wide; she could forget how puffy they were and how they ached. "You know the coast," she said carefully. "Nothing very exciting."

"What happened?" Doris stretched out across the foot of the bed, arching her back, curling her bare toes in the air. "You do look like the wrath of God."

"I can't help that," Joan said.

"Who's over there?" Doris leered. "You've been knocking yourself out with somebody."

"How do you figure that?"

"Some things Aurelie said."

Aurelie, Aurelie, Joan thought, you are so clever. You take such wonderful care of your children. Even Doris won't know. You did it all so beautifully. . . .

"You always did like secrets," Doris was saying. "Pity you won't tell me. Might even be somebody I know."

"Little sister," Joan said, "there are some people in

this world cleverer than you, some people who can run rings around you."

Doris got up, the robe falling in tangles around her feet. "Not you, old duck."

"No," Joan said truthfully. "I wasn't even thinking of me."

That afternoon she called Michael.

"Hello," she said quietly, casually. "I'm glad I caught you at home."

A pause while he identified her voice. Then a quick breath. "For God's sake," he said, "what happened to you?"

"Did you try to call me here?"

"No," he admitted, "but you said you'd call."

"Look," she said. "It's all right."

"You mean you were wrong?"

"No," she said, "but it's all right now."

"For God's sake."

The silence was so long she began to wonder. "You aren't angry?"

"Me?" he said, "I think it's terrific."

It seemed to her that she ought to say good bye and hang up. There didn't seem to be anything more. She felt awkward, as if she'd used the wrong fork.

"It was the sensible thing to do," she said finally.

"You're damn right it was," he said. "But I didn't think gals had that much sense."

What he said was true. Most gals would have wanted

to get married. Maybe she should have gotten married. Then Michael was saying something else. "I didn't hear you," she apologized.

He laughed and she recognized the old sound, crisp and open and jolly. And free.

She realized suddenly that he had been afraid. He had. And that struck her as funny. "You were afraid."

"No," he said huffily, "I wouldn't say that. But I wasn't very happy about things."

"Silly," she giggled, "silly, silly."

"Yea," he said, "I guess so."

For the very first time a conversation with him was going right. She felt good about it. She felt she was in control. And she was. All because of a tiny speck of a child.

"Tell you what," he said finally, "this deserves some sort of a celebration, don't you think?"

A celebration. Or a funeral. "Be fun," she said aloud.

"What about tomorrow?"

"It's a good day."

"We'll go have dinner at the Blue Room."

"Swell," she said, "a proper celebration."

The next day a corsage came for her—white orchids. She was very dressed up: a new dress that she had bought the previous year on vacation in Jamaica—all heavy tropical greens and blues. She felt a little light-headed, a little dizzy. She wondered if she wasn't catching something; she took her temperature and then swallowed a couple of aspirins for good measure.

In the club's dimness, he looked even more handsome than she remembered. Narrow head, thin face. Indian-looking, almost, with high cheekbones and deep shadows under them. She felt lovely; she wondered if she was. He hadn't said; he never said a word. He had never given her a compliment.

The tips of the white orchids brushed her cheek—it didn't matter. This was Now, she thought, and have fun.

"Thank you for the celebration," she said.

He took her hand across the table. "You were great," he said, "so we ought to have a party."

"A birthday party," she said.

He looked startled. "Sure if you like."

A bottle of sparkling Burgundy came. And quite suddenly she thought of Aurelie's decision: sparkling Burgundy is vulgar.

"Poor Aurelie," she said aloud.

"I guess she knew all about it."

"Oh sure," Joan said, "she didn't mind. Not really."

"For God's sake." He lifted his glass. "Here's . . ."

"Happy times," Joan said.

Later still they went down to Pat O'Brien's, to a gay noisy airless room where two pianists belted out a succession of indistinguishable songs. She ordered a gin and tonic.

"Hell," Michael said, "you want a Hurricane."

She shrugged. "I'll get drunk."

"So you get drunk. So what?"

She nodded. Right again. If she got drunk—what could happen? Nothing more can happen. Not to me.

Joan could feel the man at the next table staring at her, admiringly. The dress was good, the flowers were good, and she had done her hair properly for once. . . . It was very thrilling. That's what came of not being born pretty, she thought. You worked on it hard, and you were a lot more grateful. A lot more. More than Doris, for one. But Doris wasn't exactly pretty, either, she had something else. It must be fun. Or something like that. Life, maybe.

And without wanting to, Joan thought: but I had life too, right in my belly; after a while it would have begun to move and stir; and now I'm empty and quiet. . . .

Michael was tapping her arm. "Hi, honey bunch."

She smiled. "I was a million miles off."

"I know."

"Sorry."

"I hope you're not going to be one of those sad-type drinkers."

"I don't know."

A red-faced drunk staggered by their table, changed his mind and sat down. They both giggled at him. And he began a long rambling account of his oil wells in Texas. Finally, in the middle of a sentence, he lurched away.

Michael was chuckling, deep in his throat, quietly.

"Do you suppose he was telling the truth?" Joan asked.

"God knows."

"If this is a party," Joan said, "I would like another drink."

"Anything you want, honey bunch," Michael said. "God, you were terrific. If it had come out, I'd be fired so fast I wouldn't even see the door slamming."

"Oh," she said, "oh."

"Well sure. . . . Things like that just don't happen in the academic world."

"Well," Joan said, "it's all right."

"I'll drink on that," Michael said. "I'll get us a drink."

The room got more crowded. There was more noise, but it actually seemed quieter to Joan. The din had all subsided to an even low level roar. Far off and steady like a waterfall. She recognized the signs; she was getting very drunk.

When, several hours later, they left, she noticed that her heels weren't too steady on the broken flagstone that formed the sidewalk. She found herself staring down, selecting each stone carefully. Michael did not take her arm. He walked quietly right next to her and a little distance off.

In the car he said: "Let's go one more place."

"Sure," she said. "Where?"

"Fairy joint. Out at the lake."

I don't want to go to the lake, she thought. I've been to the lake with you. And it was a terrible time.

Aloud she said: "Sure, let's try."

It was a long drive to the lake, and the top stayed up. Just as well, she thought, the set would stay in her hair.

The other bar was small and dark and not very crowded. They had a couple of beers and watched the show.

Maybe it was the mixture of drinks, and maybe it was the mixture of sexes, but Joan began to feel very confused. She couldn't tell men from women any more.

A short slender dark-haired woman, with beautifully kept hair, and a very revealing beige dress, slipped past them on clopping heels. She touched Joan's shoulder briefly, softly. Slipped an arm into Michael's, hugged him. Then slipped away.

Michael grinned. "Now what was that?"

"I don't know."

"Man or woman, guess!"

"I can't," Joan said.

"No opinion at all?"

"Do you?"

"I know."

"Tell me?"

He shook his head.

"That's not fair." The quick alcoholic tears were very near the surface.

"What was it?"

It would be silly to cry, she told herself. And she stared determinedly down into the brown bottom of her beer bottle. "I couldn't care less." She yawned elaborately. "I'm getting awfully sleepy and tomorrow is awfully close and I can't sleep all morning."

"If it makes you feel better, I've got an eight o'clock class scheduled for the coming term."

"Eight o'clock," she said. "God!"

"Nobody would take it and it got wished on me."

"Have fun."

The road was very unsteady under her feet. The crunch of gravel seemed fantastically loud, seemed to boom out in the dark. She wondered if Michael could drive, all the stories of drunks at the wheel coming back to her with a rush. She took one quick look—he seemed to be driving with more concentration than usual, but he seemed to be doing all right.

So she leaned her head back and fell to following her own thoughts around and around. They weren't making much sense—even she could tell that. But very slowly one fact detached itself and stood out clearly. It was strange, in a way, that it hadn't appeared earlier. She wanted him. Badly. She could feel her body twisting and lifting to that imaginary shape.

Damn, she thought, oh God damn.

Then they were home, and she walked up the front

walk with her legs burning and the familiar trembling on the back of her tongue.

She fumbled with the lock. He took the key and opened it. Automatically she stepped inside. He patted her cheek, roughly. Then he was walking back down toward the car. She could tell by his walk that he was very drunk.

She called out after him: "Happy birthday."

SHE climbed the stairs. She was a little surprised to find her legs working so smoothly. She stared down at her knees rising and falling under the cloth of her skirt as they pumped her steadily up.

Without a sign from her they stopped working. She was startled and looked around. At the top, of course. How silly not to notice. She moved down the dark hall and it seemed to her that she walked several inches above the floor. She seemed to be drifting or sailing before a silent wind.

If I took off my clothes, she thought, I'd be light as paper and I'd blow about.

She felt her waist to be sure her clothes were firmly anchored there.

Once safely inside her room she dragged a chair over to the window and watched the September dawn slip up the sky. Horizon rise, she thought. And she turned her head sideways on her bent arms and rested on the sill.

She was very drunk and things didn't keep still. The soft muted colors of the earth and sky blended and shifted. Once she felt her stocking run, felt the little tickling down her leg.

I ought to undress, she told herself.

But she was very comfortable, so she didn't move.

In the quiet, even at this distance, she could hear the trickling of the water on the tiles of the fountain in the front yard.

I ought to be worried about my dress, she thought, and my girdle ought to be pinching me.

But it wasn't, so she kept very still and watched. After a couple of hours the alcoholic whirling stopped and she could make out the trees and their leaves as individual shapes and not just blobs of color. And the sky changed from a soft deep blue to the brilliant color of the coming day.

She wondered what it had been like for poor Mr. Norton, living upstairs, opening his windows each morning on the whisky-streaked world. Poor funny man. She had scarcely bothered saying hello to him.

She found herself listening for the familiar sounds, knowing that she wouldn't hear them, knowing that the upstairs attic rooms were empty.

She was going to have a terrible hang-over. That was for sure.

The sun was up strong and clear and falling into her eyes so that she had to blink and rouse herself. She got up then, very slowly. And looked at the white orchids

in the hard light—they were limp and brown. She
tucked them over her dressing-table mirror. Now the
room would smell faintly of dead flowers, faintly like a
funeral.

A funeral, she thought and said aloud, "Happy birthday."

She undressed slowly, standing in a patch of sunlight.
Both her legs had gone to sleep, from the long hours in
the chair. And they hurt. She moved about, slowly and
deliberately increasing the pain. Until it too was finished and she was left standing in the same patch of
sun (stronger and whiter now). She finished undressing
and stood watching her body in the mirror, watching
the shape and the color of the skin and the deep red
marks that bra and girdle had left.

She crinkled her nose at herself. It takes so long to
grow back, she thought; I didn't know they were going
to have to shave there. But I didn't know anything
about it. And anyway as soon as the hair grows back,
there won't be a mark to show that it ever happened.
Not a mark. And nobody will know. And nobody will
be able to tell.

But it doesn't look nice now. It looks dirty and sick
somehow, as if there were a disease. Or it looks a little
like a mangy dog.

And it's no wonder Michael didn't want to come to
bed with me, and me looking like this. He must know
how I would look.

I wonder how long it will take. And this is so silly.

I wonder if he knew I wanted him as much as I did. I wouldn't like him to know.

And it's so silly. Body running away with you like this. Running you so fast you can't sleep. And all you can think of is the mark of a man. The stupid silly mark of a man.

I'm not making sense, she told herself, I'm really not making sense.

The sun was high now. There were stirring sounds in the street and a far-off rumble of traffic on St. Charles Avenue, punctuated by the sharp clank of streetcar bells. Clara came in, letting the screen slam behind her, and began rattling dishes in the kitchen.

Familiar sounds. She had heard them a thousand times before.

Now she could walk over to the bed. She stretched out on top of the spread. Her body was sore all over, no, not sore exactly, but tender, sensitive, and she seemed to be burning. White hot, flesh hot.

SEPTEMBER was ending in its usual way, with sharp gusts of wind and grey sheets of rain. On the porches, leaves were jammed through screens like vegetables through a sieve. There were the usual hurricanes in the Gulf, hurricanes heading for the Texas coast. Once one passed so close that the gigantic neon clock advertising Jax beer (on lower St. Charles Avenue) got ripped off like a top-heavy flower. Coming down, it squashed two or three people, happy drunks who had come out of a nearby bar and were watching to see it fall.

Between the storms were periods of brilliant Caribbean sunlight. Where everything shone with a desperate hard brightness, and the frenzied autumn growth shot forward. The golden-rain trees shook their hideous pink seed pods over the walks, and camphor trees dropped their greasy black berries. Some few superstitious people still sneaked out when the moon was right and picked up the camphor berries and sewed them in a little plain cotton bag; they wore them pinned on their slips and undershirts as a sure cure against fevers.

Joan picked up a handkerchief-full and brought them into her room and left them spread out in a little wrinkling black line on the back of her dressing table, the scent mingling with the soft fragrance of the perfumes Aurelie gave her every Christmas and every birthday.

She liked the way the scents clashed. It made the nights more comfortable somehow, when she woke and in the dark could almost feel the struggle of the camphor and the perfumes.

Mr. Norton left the hospital. He came to the front and rang the doorbell, as if he had never been in the house before. Aurelie was not home; Joan answered.

"Good afternoon, my dear." He looked very well. His skin, which was always very fair, had a healthy pink cast to it. His eyes behind the gold-rimmed glasses were very bright blue. He had gained weight and his cheeks were round and full; one had a dimple. "I've come to pack a few things," he said. "Just a bag or two this time. I'll come back for the rest."

He climbed the steep stairs, patiently, stopping halfway up to catch his breath.

Not more than half an hour later he and the cab driver were carrying down three large suitcases. They had been hastily and carelessly packed. Bits of material stuck out; a plaid shirt sleeve dangled loosely and dragged along the floor. "Good bye, my dear," Mr. Norton said as they passed Joan. The suitcases made slight clinking sounds. Mr. Norton was taking his liquor supply with him.

That week too, Doris fell madly in love with a handsome Australian painter, whose name was Troy, who had wavy red hair, sun-browned skin, a thick red mustache, and an Oxford accent. He had a French Quarter apartment where the walls were painted black and the floor yellow and all the furniture was covered with a thick soft stuff like the skins of black lambs. He was also forbidden.

Aurelie had ruled him unacceptable after their first meeting. Her objection was simple. She announced it very quietly to Doris: "When my daughters go out on a date, they go with a man, not a fairy."

"I know all about that," Doris said. "Anyhow he's a bisexual."

"You are not to see him again."

"They're the best kind in bed," Doris teased. "Oh Mother . . ."

Aurelie's eyebrows lifted and she held up a single finger. She did not say anything. Even Doris was silenced by the angry look in her eyes.

Aurelie, who knew everybody and spent long hours on the phone, heard within a week that Doris and Troy were dating secretly.

Aurelie never made scenes. Joan noticed nothing wrong until Doris banged into her room. It was the

middle of the afternoon. Joan was by the window, paint-
ing in the brilliant afternoon light. She had given up
her sketching pad in favor of an easel and small bits of
canvas. Joan sighed, put her palette on the window
sill, and took off the tennis cap she wore as an eyeshade.

"God," Doris said, "that's mine."

"It's not," Joan said. "What's chasing you?"

"That son of a bitch!"

"Who?"

"Aurelie."

"In that case just plain bitch'll do."

Doris threw herself down into the armchair, shaking
a little side table as she did. A pack of cigarettes spilled
to the floor.

"What happened to you?"

"God damn."

All of a sudden Joan remembered. "Somebody told
her, huh?"

"I'd kill them," Doris said softly, "if I knew who."

"It wasn't me," Joan shrugged. "What'd she do?"

"No allowance."

"None?"

Doris nodded. Under the deep sunburn her fair skin
flushed in spots, like damp blotches on a plaster wall.
So that's what she's going to look like when she gets
old, Joan thought suddenly. She's going to be one of
those ruddy-faced old women who look tipsy all the
time.

Aloud she asked, "For how long?"

"Indefinite."

Joan nodded her head thoughtfully. "That's tough."

"You're god-damn right."

"Charge accounts?"

"I didn't ask," Doris said, "but I'd be willing to bet she fixed those too."

"She's going to pay for college, isn't she?"

"A check for tuition made out to the college."

"This one really did it, huh?"

"Look," Doris said, "you don't know the half of it. I'm supposed to play at Atlanta this coming week end."

"A tournament or something?"

Doris tossed herself about in the chair, so hard that the wood squeaked. "I can take it without any trouble. I'm bound to."

"Why'd you go with him?"

"Who?"

"The guy. What's-his-name?"

Doris shrugged. "How'd I know she'd flip like this? But I've got to go. I'll die if I don't go."

"Sounds to me like Aurelie really means this one."

"You're telling me." Doris pulled her knees up to her chin and examined them carefully. "And today I stumbled and skinned myself good on the courts. You wouldn't like to lend me some money?"

"If I had any money," Joan said, "I'd have taken a vacation."

"God damn it," Doris said, "you've got to have money."

"Don't take it out on me," Joan said, "you're supposed to be fighting with Aurelie."

"I picked my father wrong," Doris said quietly to the chandelier. "What I need is a nice rich crook like my sister's old man."

"He wasn't a crook."

"That isn't what the tax people said."

Joan knew she would give her the money. It had happened too often before for her not to know what was going to happen now. She gave up with a little sigh. "A house full of bitches."

"And that," Doris said triumphantly, "is just exactly what I've been saying."

"How much?"

Doris was rummaging around the top drawer of the desk. "Here it is." She pulled out a checkbook.

"How much?"

"A couple hundred." She was turning the pages studying the stubs. "Say," she said, "doesn't tell how much you've got."

"I'll have to call Robert D'Antoni and ask him."

"Call him right now."

He had been her father's lawyer, a short pudgy man with great rolls of wrist fat showing under his cuffs and swollen fingers that could scarcely hold a pen. He hated Aurelie with a quiet determination and had no use for her children, excepting always Joan. He enforced the provisions of Mitchell's will with grim satisfaction. He and Aurelie fought fiercely—first face-to-face, then on the phone, and finally, when they could no longer bear each other, by letter. He and Joan had lunch once a month, a quiet ritual, a memorial to her father.

"No," Joan said, "I don't have to call him. I'm sure I've got that much."

"I can hardly wait to see Aurelie's face when she finds out I'm going."

Joan wrote the check. "I wonder how much you owe me by now."

"Ask D'Antoni. . . . God he hates us."

"I suppose he does."

"Hell, old duck," Doris said, "we're all living off your old man."

"I know."

Doris folded the check and put it in the pocket of her shirt. "It really is a house full of bitches."

"I know," Joan said.

For the brief period between the closing of summer camp and the opening of school, Aurelie's daughters all came home. Joan met two of them in the hall—Phyllis and Celine. They were twelve and fourteen and had grown so over the summer she scarcely recognized them.

"When did you all get in?"

"Last night." They had been at camp together and they had got in the habit of giggling and talking together, like the twins in *Alice's Adventures in Wonderland*. "We didn't see you at dinner last night."

"I wasn't there," Joan said.

It was one of her new habits. She no longer ate dinner at home. Or if she did, she ate very early or very late—after even Clara had gone and the kitchen was empty.

All the sisters were home for a week; the house rattled and banged with their presence. Then they were gone. Only the two oldest, Doris and Joan, remained, and the house settled down. "All these girls," Aurelie said aloud to the quiet house, "how can I ever manage to pay for all these weddings?"

Because she was lonesome and feeling the subtle tugs of age, Aurelie made peace with Doris. It had come upon her so suddenly. One morning she was looking in the mirror applying make-up—and there it was, her face staring back at her. The lines that had always been there but she had not noticed them, not really. And the eyelids that were beginning to be just a bit puffy and a little too dark. And the beaked French nose that was a bit narrower and already a good bit like a corpse's sharp bill—she shuddered and told herself firmly to stop.

She went on with her make-up, methodically, because she never allowed anything to stop her routine. But she felt slightly nauseated and quite afraid. To cheer herself up, she made a series of appointments at the very best beauty salon.

She also forgave Doris and restored her tiny allowance when she started back to college. Joan registered too, though she hadn't really been sure she wanted to. Still when the day came, she found herself walking over, studying the catalogue and filling out the forms.

She didn't take a regular degree course. She picked her courses at random, and kept choosing them until her schedule was filled.

She wasn't interested. It was just something to do. While waiting.

She thought of that sometimes. Waiting for what? And she didn't have an answer. Even for herself.

Sometimes it seemed that she was waiting for the telephone to ring. She would find herself awake at night, listening hard. And sometimes she would pick up the instrument and listen to the steady buzz on the other end.

She got asked to resign from her sorority. She had forgotten to go to three meetings. Aurelie was distressed. "That's ridiculous," she said. "I belonged to that sorority and you're not going to resign."

Joan shrugged.

"I was a founding member," Aurelie said heatedly. "They can't do this."

Aurelie stalked off to her room and put in long-distance calls to the proper people.

Joan watched her go, with a tiny smile on her lips. Then she went up to her room, got out her typewriter and pounded out with two fingers her resignation:

Having learned in your organization the virtues and merits of the capitalist system, I now resign. Since I have only a certain sum of money for membership dues, I must resign from your club and use that money to join the Communist Party. It is slightly more expensive, but will I feel be well worth it as an investment in the future.

She signed the letter, and glanced at it again. It sounds crazy, she thought, and it is crazy. And what in God's name am I talking about. There must be something wrong with me. I've never heard of anybody in my family who was crazy before. But that isn't the sort of thing they'd be likely to tell you. And I wonder.

And the funniest thing of all is that I liked belonging to the sorority. I like it. And it was fun. And I don't want to stop just because I forgot some meetings.

But Aurelie can fix it up. Aurelie always knows the right people. Aurelie can fix it. Daughters of founding members don't get thrown out, no matter what they do. Aurelie will have it all fixed by tomorrow. And everybody will forget it. Aurelie knows so many people. Fix up anything. And what do they do with the little shrimp child? Red and stringy. What do they do? Do they bury it? But you couldn't do that. It isn't a person. The grave of a shrimp, the grave of a seaweed. What to put on the marker? And that would be silly.

So down the toilet.

And this stupid letter, this stupid silly letter.

Aurelie could fix it. Could fix it all.

She read the letter again, carefully. Then sealed it, and made a special trip to the corner to mail it.

A couple of days later Aurelie glared at Joan over her breakfast grapefruit. "I don't really know what to think. Why didn't you tell me you wanted to resign?"

"You found out," Joan said, sadly. "You always find out."

"While I'm working hard as I can, you ruin the entire thing."

"I don't know why I wrote that."

"Why?" Aurelie clutched the front of her green housecoat closer over her bosom. "My dear child, I am beginning to think there must be insanity somewhere in your father's family."

"I thought of that," Joan said.

"I wash my hands of it," Aurelie said, "the whole horrible thing."

"That's all right," Joan said, "I don't mind really. Not much. Not really."

"*Mon Dieu!*" Aurelie said.

"Don't feel bad about it."

From the startled look on Aurelie's face Joan saw that she had profoundly surprised her—for the very first time in her life.

THE last days of September passed. Joan went to classes occasionally. She could see the way the other students looked at her now—a mixture of amusement and annoyance. A nut: they thought clearly. She shrugged and paid no attention. She scarcely talked to anyone, even people she had known long before. She still had her job in the library and she spent long hours on the top level of the stacks, alone, painfully reading book after book, not knowing a day later just what she had read.

She had not seen Fred Aleman for several weeks. She had been out with him only once since her return from the coast. He called, regularly three times a week, but she still found excuses not to go out.

"My telephone friend," he called her, and she knew that he was not joking. Still, she put off the inevitable. And she really did enjoy the long bantering conversations. She just did not want to see him. She was relaxed and at ease on the phone. Face to face she was afraid.

She did not think about the future. She did not allow herself to.

Late one afternoon she was leaving the library—earlier than usual because she was hungry. She had forgotten to have lunch. As she was halfway out of the Gothic door, she stopped, blinking into the light.

She could see only the silhouette for a moment. But she knew that; she would recognize that anywhere. "Fred," she said, "I thought you'd be working."

"I came up to catch you, if that's the only way I can do it."

He took her arm and steered or pulled her into his car that was double-parked just outside.

"I was going over to get a hamburger or something."

"No lunch?"

She shook her head.

"I'll take you over to the Azalea Grill."

They drove silently. Still silently they slipped into the bright red lacquered booth.

Finally Joan said: "I'm still sort of dazed. I was so busy working." She had a second's private panic as she realized that she could not recall the title of the book she had just been reading.

He didn't question her. And she relaxed, smiled a little and felt better. "It's a real pleasant surprise, though," she said.

The hamburger came; she doused hers with onions and relish and bit into it eagerly.

"You really were hungry."

"Sure," she said.

He had only coffee; he sugared it carefully and stirred it slowly. "Finish up your food, little animal, then I want to talk to you."

In less than five minutes she was done. "I wasn't hungry, I was starving."

"Okay," he said, "now listen to me."

"Before or after dessert?" she grinned.

"Be serious now." He was staring right at her and she felt the same squirming sensation she always felt when confronted with directness.

"I'm serious."

"I think I've been an idiot," he said levelly, his eyes unblinking.

His eyes fascinated her the way dark eyes always did: they were mirrors, they were surfaces, they were deep cones that went back to a tiny point that was where he lived. A tiny point way back in the middle of his head.

"A god-damn idiot not to put some things together."

"How?" she asked because she felt she had to say something.

"When you went to the coast," he asked steadily, "were you pregnant?"

Why does he have to be so direct, she thought. Why ask? If he knows.

"That was a long time ago," she dodged.

"So you were."

"This is silly."

"Don't you think you could have asked me something about it?"

He thinks it's his . . . and maybe it is. Maybe. Just maybe. Stranger things have happened. And it doesn't matter whose it was. Because it's gone. It wasn't anybody's but mine, and it's gone.

"I went off for a little vacation," she said, "just because I was tired. It wasn't anything so dramatic."

"It fits," he said, "it all fits. You were kind of strange before you left, and you've been very strange since you came back."

"How strange?"

"Withdrawn. . . . Like you were waiting for something."

So he'd noticed it too. . . . And what was she expecting? What was it? "I don't mean to be strange or anything."

"You little idiot, why didn't you ask me?"

"There wasn't anything to ask."

He went back to his coffee, stirring the weak brown liquid slowly about.

"Looks like you're about to poach an egg in that," she said irrelevantly.

"Well," he said wryly to the coffee cup, "you've got courage for one thing."

"No," she said, "I'm an awful coward."

"But you didn't have to."

"There wasn't anything to do."

"But you wouldn't have done it if you hadn't wanted to, I guess. . . ."

"I didn't do anything. Anything at all," she repeated patiently.

He wasn't listening to her. He was thinking out loud. Thinking old thoughts. Thoughts he had run through the projector of his mind so often they were fraying at the edges and the words were memorized and familiar.

"I guess that wasn't any way to start. . . . So I guess you were right."

She drank her water slowly, only half listening to him.

"You gave yourself a pretty awful beating, you know. You look tired. And older."

"It's the weather," she said. "I hate this weather."

"It took me a long time to put things together, when it shouldn't have. But I am sorry."

"Look," she said, "everything's fine. Nothing's wrong. Nothing at all."

"Sure," he said. "Do you want to go home?"

"No," she said, "just drop me off at the library."

THE following week Joan bought herself a car, a secondhand black Pontiac.

"My dear," Aurelie said with horror when she saw it, "you're not going to leave it parked out front?"

"Where else? when we haven't got a garage."

"Couldn't you park it farther down the street?"

"Okay, okay, I'll move it."

Doris looked at it carefully. "And I had to pull teeth to get two hundred," she said softly. "Rich bitch."

After that first day Joan kept the car parked around the corner. And in a way she preferred that. For no one at the house knew when she drove away. Not that it mattered whether they knew or not. They would never have thought of stopping her.

But they might have asked idly, to make conversation, "What are you doing, where are you going?"

And questions would spoil things. Joan floated—not happily, but not unhappily either—suspended in space, unhampered, able to move at will. Like water, she liked to think.

The secrecy was necessary to her. She wanted to move without anyone knowing she was moving. She wanted to slip like a ghost through walls. That was one of her recurring fantasies—that she was a ghost and slid through doors and slid through trees and crept into houses and watched what happened there. (For with this new urge of hers went a great curiosity—a curiosity about little things, about details of living.)

She had taken to leaving by the back steps, the narrow twisting flight that not even Clara used any more. The single overhead light had long since burned out and nobody bothered to replace it. She had to feel her way, carefully, her arms stretched out on both sides of her, palms resting on the walls to guide her down.

One day she was absolutely startled to meet Aurelie with Doris, flashlight in hand, coming up.

"Mercy sakes," Aurelie said, "you'll break your neck, child, without a light."

Joan backed up again without a word and let them come up. The stair was far too narrow to pass.

"Were you going through in the dark?" Aurelie asked.

Joan just nodded.

"Cat's eyes," Doris giggled.

Aurelie shrugged. "Don't break your neck. And by the way it will be about half an hour before the steps are dry."

"Sure," Joan said, "sure thing."

It was not until she was groping her way down that she realized what had happened. They had waxed the regular stairs. Of course. She could smell the crisp sharp odor of the wax; she had been smelling it all along without noticing.

And they thought she had noticed. So they did not know. She was so relieved that she stopped in the middle of her groping and grinned triumphantly to herself. They still did not know that she used this way regularly. They still did not know. . . .

She felt like laughing. She felt like sitting right down and laughing.

She still had her way out. She had slipped it by their very noses. She was still free. To come and go unnoticed. In secret.

Not that she knew why. . . . She didn't bother to ask herself that. It just was and that was all.

She kept her job in the library, asking for the late hours that none of the staff wanted. She liked the quiet still emptiness, where each step, however carefully rubber-cushioned, echoed right through the building. She liked the way—at closing—the lights went out, tier after tier, first the stack lights, then the reading rooms, and last of all the corridors. She found she could move just ahead of them, as she would have done before a coming tide.

She would stand at the door of the stacks until those lights blinked and disappeared. She would move to the door of the reading rooms and wait the five minutes there. Then, moving slowly, she would time herself to be just at the front door when the hall lights blinked out.

She rarely missed. When she did, she corrected the timing by a few seconds' conversation with the watchman who stood waiting to lock up.

She would find herself going down the wide outside steps, in the soft warm fall night. She would go down them without any hesitation, because she knew them so well. And she would turn down the sidewalk, walking slowly to her car. She always parked several blocks away, deliberately. She walked slowly, purse swinging idly in her left hand, her heels making tiny sounds on the cement. She followed the paths through the dark buildings, paths lit by only an occasional light standard. She made her walk as long as possible: she liked the feel of the dark, of the little night wind, of the smell of the earth, the leaf mold cooling after a day's heat, of all these things around her. And her alone.

She rather liked being alone, it gave her a sharp clear feeling. This is me, she could say to herself in the dark, and for the first time she would know exactly what she meant. She did not have to figure herself in relation to other people now.

And in the dark—on the shadowy benches, in the doorways of the Gothic buildings—she could hear the quick shuffling and shifting of the couples as she passed. Sometimes, because her ears were sharp, she could hear their whispers off in the distance, sharp hushed little whispers—before they heard her steps and fell silent for her to pass.

Sometimes, hidden by a tree, she would stand stock-still and listen. As if she were hunting. Listen until the small sounds of the warm night came back. And it seemed to her then that the whole dark was full of couples, the building, the bushes, the shrubs, the trees, even the leaves overhead. Soft wet sounds.

That stopped when she moved again.

When she finally got to her car she would snap on the radio and see her hand outlined in the little light from the dash. And she would feel clear and hard and definite.

It was a very comfortable feeling.

Though it would then be a few minutes past eleven, she rarely went directly home. Instead she went driving. The car had given her a feeling of new mobility and looseness. She did not care particularly where she went. She chose streets because she liked the way they looked. One night she turned down only the widest avenues, palm-fringed and littered by the falling seeds of tremendous golden-rain trees. Another night she drove along the narrowest and darkest back streets, dirt rutted, littered with cans, where Negro faces peered at her and she tried to hide her white nakedness.

She rarely got home before three. Usually too she stopped off at the Azalea Grill for a hamburger. Without thinking she would find that her circling ended in front of its chromium counters, and she would come blinking from the dark into the brilliant blue fluorescent glare.

One afternoon, in the very first weeks of October, she had just wakened and was stretching idly in bed, when Fred called her. They chattered a bit. Though she was aware of something else in his voice, she was too sleepy to isolate it.

Finally he asked directly, "Should I call you again?"

She was startled. "What?"

"Would you be happier if I didn't call you again?"

"I don't know," she said, imitating a yawn, and stalling for time. "I just woke up."

He was not going to be put off. "Would you miss it if I didn't call you again?"

And she very deliberately said something that wasn't true. "I guess not," she said, "I guess I wouldn't."

"That's what I wanted to know," he said quietly. And hung up.

She put the receiver back carefully and sat on the edge of the bed for quite some time, wondering: why did I say that? When I know it isn't true. Why did I? Why did I want to hurt myself?

She was learning to look upon herself as a separate person. She found herself observing her activities, being a little surprised with each discovery. She regarded herself with interest and detachment, as if she were a strange zoo specimen of whose behavior she did not entirely approve.

She found herself watching for Michael Kern. She had already done it several times before she realized what she was doing.

Often during her night prowls she would pull to the curb, leaving the motor running, and listen to the empty streets or the sound of the lake. It was just one of the things she did. It did not particularly matter to her where she was. Most times she did not notice.

But this one time, a wet gusty night, she looked out of the window and read the number of the yellow stucco apartment building she had stopped by. She had never seen it before. It was on a side street facing a little park. The number was familiar; she stared at it: 4608. Done in flowing curving iron letters over the iron-barred door.

She remembered. She had called Michael Kern just twice. She had looked him up in the phone book. Both times. 4608 Villere Street. That was it. She had remembered without knowing it.

She went over and glanced at the names over the long line of bells. She found his without any trouble. There was still mail jammed in the box. Which meant he was not home yet. She scurried off hastily, and back in the dark safety of the car realized that her hair was dripping cold streams of water down her neck. She had forgotten to use an umbrella.

She sat very quietly for a few minutes. Until she saw a Ford convertible slide into place at the side of the building. And a hunched figure dash for the door. She was not sure who it was, until he stopped and fumbled for his mail, holding a cigarette lighter as he unlocked the box.

Then he was gone into the depths of the building. She waited patiently to see what light went on. The third floor on the left side. It wasn't a very deep building. All the apartments must run from front to back, so their rooms would be strung out in a long straight line. Like a shotgun house, she thought, only an apartment instead.

And what was it like inside? She wished she had seen it. Now she wished she had. What were the rooms like? How many were there? Were they furnished with the usual wicker and chintz, or did he bring his own stuff? And were the owls still there? Or had he sent them on to his aunt? The owls, the stuffed owls. . . .

She shook her head and drove off quickly.

A couple of nights later she was back at the same place, knowing now how she had come there. The lights inside were on this time; the curtains weren't drawn, though it was too high to see. She studied the two bars of light, blurred in the drizzle. Yellow radiance in the mist, little glow like yellow smoke, drifting out.

After about ten minutes she saw him come out. This time he wasn't alone. There was somebody with him, somebody tall, wearing a bright green raincoat. Whose high heels clattered as they ran across the rain-soaked sidewalk.

When they were gone, she stared into the splattered windshield.

Drops, dribbles, drops, dribbles, she thought nonsensically. Dribble dribble toil and tribble.

And she laughed out loud at herself.

She sat very still, letting her eyes see the patterns of dark and light, not thinking of anything at all. Drifting. Like seaweed.

She wouldn't go to the beach any more. Just to the mountains. Where there were sleek green fish in shallow stony streams. . . .

She didn't notice until the flashlight touched her face. She saw the shiny black raincoat first, then the shiny visor and the shiny badge.

"You in trouble, lady?"

Then she saw the prowl car pulled in right behind her.

"Goodness," she said, "you startled me."

"You in trouble?"

"No," she said, "mercy no."

"Look," he said, "it's not exactly the safest place, alone in a car. Things happen."

She smiled her best finishing-school smile. "That's why I leave my motor running."

The officer shook his head. "Sounds kind of crazy to me."

She chuckled softly. "It is."

"Why this block and this same spot?"

"I guess you noticed me here before."

He nodded.

"Before I get myself shot for a suspicious character . . ." Her voice trailed off as she thought of the proper words to use. The man was waiting patiently. She couldn't see his face. "Look," she said, "it's like this. I had a boyfriend and we broke up, not much more than a couple of months ago. Not that much. I've been waiting to see if there was a chance for me. Until tonight he's come home alone. Only tonight there was a girl up there. So I know he's got a girl. And that's what I wanted to find out."

The harsh rough words she had used made her feel better. Things cleared and shifted back into a sharper focus. Being tough and cheap made her feel happier. She lived for the moment in a world where such things happened all the time, were a part of life and nobody noticed. Nobody thought anything of it.

"Look," the policeman said, "go on home."

"I will," she said, "but I'll be back. Maybe not tomorrow, but soon. So you'll know."

"Lady," he said patiently, "take it easy."

"No guns. . . . Anyhow, he ought to be nibbled to death by ducks." She giggled. "But I want to find out who she is."

"Okay," the man said, "okay."

"Nothing wrong in that. Perfectly legal."

"Sure," he said. "Don't let it get out of hand."

"I'm not exactly the type who goes wading around in blood up to my knees."

"You never know," he said and went back to the patrol car.

That struck her as so very funny she chuckled all the way home.

She had found a way out now. Whenever she felt the quivering shaking uncertainty coming near her, she would go off by herself, where there was no one to hear. And she would say her little story out loud, using the crudest words she could think of. Sometimes she made up the images, graphic ones that struck her imagination. She told the whole thing aloud to herself. The quivering would stop and she would feel better. She would feel fine.

A week or so later, Joan saw the raincoat, the green raincoat, tossed over a chair in the ladies' room at the library. Beside it were two books. Joan recognized them as freshman English and math. She flipped one open, glanced at the name written across the flyleaf in crisp bright green ink. Then she sat down in the next chair, rummaged in her bag for a lipstick, and began methodically redoing her make-up, waiting for the owner to emerge.

She came finally, a tall thin girl, with shingled black hair and pale lipstick and heavy eyes. She slipped into the green raincoat, belted it, picked up the books. She hesitated, turned back to the mirror, snapped open her purse and ran a tiny comb through her unruffled hair. Then she checked her teeth for lipstick and, turning, checked her seams carefully.

Joan said: "I couldn't help noticing that raincoat. I think it's the loveliest I've ever seen."

The girl looked surprised, then smiled.

"I'm sure there isn't another one like it in town."

"As a matter of fact," the dark-haired girl said, "I got a dressmaker to run it up from a coat pattern."

"Do you mind . . ." Joan touched one finger to a sleeve, brushing lightly. Smooth and curiously warm. As if it held body heat.

"It's Japanese silk," the girl said.

"Good heavens," Joan persisted, "it *is* lovely."

"Well actually," the girl gathered up her books and purse again, "it isn't too practical; it isn't very waterproof and I have to race between buildings to keep from getting soaked."

And from buildings to car, Joan said silently to the closing door.

Joan went back to classes. And under the ironic glances and the wisecracking of her professors set about catching up. I'm not stupid, she told herself. I can do it.

Working so hard kept her on campus most of the time and she could see the green raincoat pass back and forth. She kept track of it. The way you'd keep track of a timber in the surf. Loosing it for long periods, seeing

it finally bob to the surface again. But you keep track-
ing it because you want to avoid it. And you always
know most about the things you have to avoid.

It drizzled for weeks. Grey days streaked by the passing of a bright green raincoat.

Without knowing it, without willing it, Joan got to
know more and more about the girl. She knew which
dormitory she lived in, that her classes ran from nine
until one, that she had a psychology lab on Wednesday afternoon. That Michael picked her up after the
lab ended at five o'clock; that they went out to supper.

That they had three dates a week, which was all
freshmen were allowed to have.

The rains stopped and the cool clear days of late
October began. The green silk raincoat disappeared.
It was harder to keep track now. Without the coat she
blended in with the other girls.

So Joan took to waiting for them. She knew the freshman curfew hours; she parked her black Pontiac at the
corner of the dormitory and waited. Whenever a
watchman passed, she slipped down in her seat and the
Pontiac was just another parked car along a public
street. Anyway, the watchmen never looked closely at
the cars: they were nearly always full of necking couples.

Afterward, she followed Michael back, saw him in
his door. She felt very protective toward him; she could
sleep better knowing that he was safely at home.

She did not bother to think about it, she did not

analyze. She only knew that after she had seen him home she was quite peaceful and curiously happy in a quiet way.

It was Aurelie who suggested the psychiatrist. She did it one morning—as things always were done in the house on Coliseum Street—at breakfast. She popped her black-framed reading glasses over the edge of the morning paper and stared straight at Joan. "Why don't you see Cousin Oliver, if you're not feeling well?"

Joan was idly squirting the juice from half-peeled sections of an orange. She was trying to outline the flower pattern on her plate. "Me?"

"If you are not feeling well," Aurelie said, "I think it would be a very good idea."

"I feel fine."

Aurelie folded the paper carefully and laid it beside her own plate. "You haven't had a date in months. You come and go all hours of the day and night."

"I happen to want to study," Joan said self-consciously. "I'm just tired of wasting my time around here."

"You come and go all hours of the night. Alone." Aurelie shook her head. "For a young girl . . . Something is wrong."

"I don't need a head shrinker," Joan said.

"Now that *is* rude."

"I'm not crazy."

"Something is bothering you."

"Just because I don't want to be a featherbrain and an idiot like all the people you know. . . ."

Aurelie shrugged. "For your sake."

"You try to lift yourself, just a little bit, and everybody around here thinks you're crazy."

"A young woman without an escort late at night," Aurelie made a face of horror.

"No escort," Joan said furiously, "and you don't have to keep fighting him off to defend your virtue."

Doris chuckled softly.

"That is quite enough," Aurelie said to her.

"I would rather not go out with the slobs around here."

"Mercy mercy," Doris said.

"Leave the table," Aurelie said. But she was looking at Joan, and Doris went on quietly finishing her breakfast.

With her finger Joan moved the orange peels into a heap in the center of the plate. "Oliver is crazy."

"He is a very brilliant man."

"Oh shit."

"That," Doris said, "is my line."

Aurelie glared at her younger daughter. "It must be my blood," she said to no one in particular. "You all had different fathers and you all came out the same way. The exact same way."

"Not like her," Doris giggled, "don't tell me I'm like her. I couldn't stand it."

Joan didn't bother answering.

"I think you should," Aurelie repeated to Joan.

"If my habits bother you," Joan said formally, "I can always leave."

Aurelie sighed. "Back to that. If your idiot of a father had had any sense he would never have left you that money outright."

"But he did," Joan said, quietly triumphant.

"He was an idiot."

"I can afford my own apartment."

Aurelie sighed. "Dramatics," she said, "I hate dramatics. Go away and let me finish my coffee in peace."

AFTER a few days Joan no longer waited for Michael at curfew time by the dormitory. She joined their evenings earlier, followed them more closely: when they met, on the walk outside Tilton Hall, she was watching. She followed them clumsily at first, then with practice more and more easily.

For the next few weeks she trailed them about the city, silently, patiently, matter-of-factly. She did not feel upset, or angry. She felt patient; as if in a way she were only doing her duty.

It seemed to her sometimes, as they formed an unknown trio, that they should leave marks in the night, like jet trails. Telltale marks. That would repeat aloud that the couple was not a couple after all. That there was a watcher.

When she thought about it, it struck her as funny that she should be so happy in her role as observer. But she did not think about it very often.

She had trouble only once. When she was waiting for

them outside the Sahara Club, parked quietly a half block away, a man in a light suit had tried to open the sidewalk-side door. It was locked; she always kept them locked. He stood rattling the handle, while she hesitated. In a sudden anger, he began kicking the door, hard. She shifted quickly, and drove off. For a few yards the man held on to the door, lifted his feet and coasted along, stuck to the side like a monkey. But as she gathered speed, he dropped off. She saw him in her mirror, standing at the side of the highway, brushing off the front of his light suit.

She drove down a bit, circled and came back. She made one quick trip through, checking to be sure that the convertible was still there. Then parked again, this time among the necking couples in the back lot. She wasn't noticed.

And when Michael came out of the door, she was waiting and followed them back.

That Saturday they went on a sailing party. Joan recognized the boat. She had been on it several times, some two years past. It was an old Biloxi lugger, rigged as a party boat. Its hull was unpainted and scuffed by years of hard use. But its deck was screened, and all the cabin partitions had been pulled out to make one large room. It wasn't seaworthy any more, but it had a very large ice chest, a very fine radio, and a more or less reliable engine.

They chugged out past the yacht club with the radio going full blast.

Joan watched them over the horizon, then, as she stared out at the thin line of lake and sky, broken now and then with the little peaks of sailboats, she realized something. She had noticed, of course she had noticed, she just hadn't understood. Until now.

During the last few days they had begun sleeping together. . . . Joan nodded to herself. She was sure. She had watched them too long and too carefully not to notice the slight difference now. A certain ease. Their figures were no longer wire tense. As they moved, they swayed gently, ever so slightly, tending together, delicately touching but not really touching.

She knew it now.

By five that afternoon it was clear that they were not coming back for supper. Joan went home.

She showered and changed into a bright yellow dress and tossed a bright yellow sweater around her shoulders, because the evenings now were cool.

She had a slow supper—alone, for the house seemed to be empty. How funny, she thought, I don't even know what they're doing any more.

She finished, piled the dishes in the sink and drove back to the lake. Freshmen, she knew, on Saturdays had the same curfew hour as everyone else in the dormitories . . . two o'clock. So the boat would be coming back around midnight. She got to the harbor at eleven.

She had figured correctly. First she heard the loud blaring of the radio and she wondered if they had bothered to turn it off at all during the long day. Then she

heard the groan and rattle and thump of the engine. Finally she saw the chipped white hull swing into the
circle of light from the clubhouse. And she heard the
noisy mixture of voices from the deck.

When the convertible pulled away she was in no
hurry to follow. She knew where they would have to be
going.

She got to the dorm a few minutes behind them; the
parking places were filled. She felt a sudden panic.
There was the convertible. She thought she could see
heads in it, but she wasn't sure. And passing so close,
she didn't dare stop. She drove past, letting the tail of
her eye catch a dark hump that might have been a couple or might have been a steering wheel, or a coat
thrown over the back of the seat.

She turned at the corner, into the campus, and found
a parking place. She popped out, hurrying along the
dark leaf-strewn and slippery walks. As she came around
the corner of the building, at the top of the little rise,
where the lawn sloped off down to the street, she saw
the convertible move off, with a brisk impatient gun-
ning of the motor.

She was out of breath; she turned back into the
shadow of the trees and sat down on one of the benches.

It was a cool night, clear and crisp. At the street entrance to the dormitory there was a flurry of cars and
flashing lights and muffled voices—as girls and their
dates rushed to make the deadline.

She did not know how long she had been sitting

there—she no longer wore a watch—but her breathing was regular now and calm. In the dormitory the lights were off too, except for the little ones burning in the lobby and along the halls.

A watchman sauntered past her, humming under his breath. In spite of her light dress, he did not see her, for the bench she had picked was half behind a thick low growth of azalea.

She sat there very quietly, thinking about nothing, listening to the night birds and the sounds of little animals moving. It was nice to be outside, and alone, when everything else was dark and sleeping. Gave you the feeling of being the only one alive in the world. Your breathing was so loud. And you held your breath to see what it was like when you weren't there.

After a bit, when she got cold, she stood up and began to walk to her car. She left the paths and cut along in the shadow of the bushes, moving noiselessly. It was a trick she had learned when she was a child, spending summers with her father. It was part of a game of Indians then, and the chauffeur, who was a redbone, half Indian and half Negro, had played patiently with her. . . . She could do it perfectly now. She left the night silence like water unruffled behind her.

THAT same night she wrote the letter. She did not remember exactly when she sat down at her small machine and typed it out. She did know that she sat very
still over it for a long while, staring at the typewriter
keys, scratching with her fingernails at the smear of
bright red nail polish along the top of the machine. The
keys had polish on them too; she had always tried to
type just when her polish was new and wet. . . .

She had carried the letter around with her for a
whole day. A long white envelope in the bottom of her
purse. Gathering lint and bits of tobacco and the scents
of different perfumes. A faint smell of leather. Edges
beginning to grey just a bit.

Then, quite suddenly, she passed a mailbox and almost without thinking, she opened her purse and
dropped in the letter. And that was that.

The letter said, in two lines: Do you think your parents would be interested in hearing that you are having
an affair with M.K.?

As she had expected, there were no more dates. She watched for a few days to be sure, and then no longer haunted the dark streets and parked alongside the dorms.

In the early days of November, steady heavy rains began as they always did, bringing in the first of the winter weather. She wore boots now and a raincoat and carried an umbrella and when she stepped through the library door, that door was snatched out of her hand. When she walked, she walked leaning against a wind. She still parked her car at the far edge of the campus and as she went along, leaves and bits of branches would be tossed down at her, pasted against her oilcloths by the force of the rain.

And where were the couples now, she wondered. Where would they go?

The rain made her feel terribly old. Old enough to be their mother. Old enough to be through with the hot drive of mating.

Old as the wet earth under her bootsoles.

She felt herself get stronger and stronger. Felt each muscle along her skeleton stretch and flex and tighten. Firmer, harder, impenetrable.

I'll never die, she thought one night as she reached her car. How could I?

Her mood changed. She was no longer impenetrable; she was light. Easy and drifting.

I can remember, she thought, when I was born. A lot of swirling waters and a beat like surf pounding.

And do you remember dying afterward? Like that. A circle. Slipping in and out of life. And did an embryo remember dying? Did my seaweed child remember? Drifting and surf pounding. . . .

Empty inside and lonesome. Caverns and caves, echoing. The Holy Ghost now. Or the Shower of Gold. . . .

Being one is so lonesome. With another heart ticking away inside. A different beat. A ragged pattern. The little ticking heart. The soft floating seaweed bones. . . .

IV. WINTER

A SUNDAY in November. The bleak bare desolate look of a southern winter. Joan had been up early, had looked out, and come back to bed. She spent the day there, not bothering to eat, listening to the soft Sunday sounds of bells and quiet traffic. Muted, not quite real sounds.

At five o'clock, when she was sure he'd be home, she called Fred Aleman. "I just wanted to apologize." She did not bother saying hello. "I've been being a monster and I'm sorry." She hung up quickly, before he could say anything.

The flowers came, as she had known they would, about an hour later. Aurelie herself brought them up. "You make up with somebody?"

"Yes," Joan said, "Fred."

"That's nice," Aurelie said vaguely. "Do you feel all right?"

Joan almost giggled at the sly eyes darting around the room, looking for some sign of disorder. "Some sort of bug," she said, "kept me still all morning."

"Oh dear," Aurelie said, "I just know it was left over from that Jamaica trip last year."

"I suppose so," Joan said politely. "Anyhow I feel kind of rocky."

"Some tea?"

"No," Joan said, "nothing." There seemed to be people coming and going in the downstairs hall. "What's going on?"

"Friends of Doris."

"Shouldn't you be down?"

"That," Aurelie said, "is not polite."

"My stomach hurts," Joan said.

Aurelie left, closing the door firmly behind her. Joan opened the long white box across the foot of her bed. Yellow roses. She called Fred back.

"Was there a card?" he asked.

For a moment she panicked; there had not been a card. "No," she said, and told the absolute truth, "but I don't know anybody else who would."

"I'm teasing you," he said. "I knew you liked yellow so I sent them."

"Can I ask you to supper," she said, "tonight?"

He hesitated for just a moment. "Sure," he said, "sure thing."

And she knew something else. That he had had another date which he was going to cancel. She felt triumphant. "Doris has the house full of screaming people," she said, "but I think it's just for cocktails. You want to make it about seven thirty so I'll have time to cook?"

"Why don't we go out instead?"

"Because."

"Because what?"

"Because," she said firmly, "I'm doing penance for being so nasty."

He chuckled. "Well," he said, "you're direct. I'll be there."

No, I'm not, she thought as she hung up. I'm devious. All sorts of things, but not direct.

She dressed carefully in a full-skirted wool print and went downstairs. She headed straight for the freezer and dug through the packages. She pulled out a pint of crawfish bisque, and a small steak. She found a package of potato puffs and a carton of green peas. She brought them back to the stove. Then because she felt suddenly hungry she fixed herself a cup of fresh coffee. There was a platter of small cocktail sandwiches on the table. She took two and ate them. She was leaning on the window sill looking out into the tiny back yard when the door swung open and Doris bounced into the room with a clatter of high heels and a swirl of bourbon.

"For God's sake," Doris said, "the dead have arisen."

"Hi," Joan said, "is it a nice party?"

"Fine party. . . . What are you doing?"

"Cooking."

Doris inspected the packages. "My God, Aurelie's

bisque. She'll kill you for using that when she's been saving it for a year in there."

Joan shrugged. "I needed it."

"You better hope Aurelie doesn't need it."

"Did she go out?"

"Yep."

"I thought I saw her all dressed up."

"Bet anything she's met somebody."

"Could be."

"Here we go again," Doris said. "Another wedding. Why doesn't she just sleep with them?"

Joan asked: "Is that crowd here for cocktails, or the evening?"

"Aurelie asked that too," Doris made a delighted face. "We're going before very long."

"Okay."

She clattered off with the platter of sandwiches.

Joan got up and put the frozen bisque on to heat. She stood watching the flame and wishing the lump in her own stomach would go away.

Fred came promptly, as he always did. The cocktail party was gone then and the house was still and empty. It was a charming house, Joan thought as the bell rang. Even the worn boards of the floor looked lovely to her, and the tall thin narrow windows looked dignified. She felt her grandparents and her great-grandparents lurking behind her, propping her up.

They sat in the living room and had Martinis. "The house looks so nice to me today," she said.

"It's a beautiful house."

"I don't always think so."

"Joan and her house on Coliseum Street," he teased.

"Anyhow," she said finally, feeling that there was more said than they were actually saying and wanting to figure it out, "come talk to me while I finish dinner."

They ate in the dining room, properly, at a carefully set lace-covered table.

"You've been to a great deal of trouble," Fred said.

"I told you why."

"Damned if you didn't."

"Anyhow I want to talk to you."

"You're so serious."

"I'm not a good cook," she said, choosing her words carefully, trying to feel out just the right approach for him, "and I don't know the first thing about housekeeping." She could see by the sudden expressionlessness on his face that he knew what was coming. "But I guess I could learn and not be too bad about it."

"I guess so." He wasn't going to help her. He wasn't going to help her at all.

So she tried directly. "You used to want to get married. A while ago. Do you still?"

"I don't get it," he said.

That persistent cold feeling. "Because I would like to get married."

He still did not say anything. He was studying the epergne in the center of the table.

"Maybe I waited too long," she said lamely, "maybe you don't want to."

He smiled at her across the table, suddenly. "It is kind of peculiar, you'll admit that."

"Don't laugh at me."

"I wasn't . . . but I always thought that women wanted more moonlight and roses in the approach."

"We've had that already."

"I'd swear you'd been married four times from the way you talk, so that the whole thing was very business-like."

"I didn't mean it to sound that way."

"Poor baby," he said, "let's go get a bottle of champagne and celebrate properly."

She nodded, biting her lower lip. For some absurd reason she said, "I feel like crying." That was true.

"Now that," Fred said, "is the only real true female reaction I have had from you all evening."

She sniffled, struggling for control.

"I guess I won't ever know what happened to you," he said evenly, "what changed your mind. But it doesn't matter. At least to me."

Then because he had come so very close to the truth and because she didn't know what else to do she broke down and cried long comforting sobs.

THE winter slipped along. Aurelie watched the weather reports carefully and at the first news of a frost rushed out to cover her camellias with quilts and blankets and pieces of plastic. In the wider lawns the grass turned brown with a frost, grew green in a week, turned brown with the next. The last cluttery seed pods of the golden-rain trees got blown along the gutters and the sidewalks by the steady east wind. Children straggling along the streets on their way to school were beginning raggedly to sing Christmas carols.

As Joan lay in bed in the mornings she could hear their monotonous chanting: "Jingle bells, jingle bells, jingle bells. . . ." Why, she thought, did they never learn any more of the words?

Each morning they sang the same thing. Each morning she thought the same thing.

She dozed pleasantly, leaning on time like a cushion. Feeling it flow like water.

It was an illusion she had sometimes, particularly in

the morning. That she floated in a current, effortlessly. Time, the everlasting river.

Things happened as she slipped along. But not to her. She could feel them happening all around her. And sometimes she turned her head and looked to see what they were.

The news of Mr. Norton was like that.

The phone call came in the middle of a cold rainy afternoon. Joan answered. It was a woman's voice, gentle, apologetic, asking for Mrs. Norton.

"I don't think she's here," Joan said. "Can I take a message?"

The voice coughed, very lightly. "Would you tell her that her husband just died?"

That was how they found out. Thin grey Mr. Norton had collapsed and died of a stroke while sitting on a bench in Jackson Square, feeding the pigeons.

He went every day, rain or clear. On this day the square was empty—it was cold and drizzling. So it was quite awhile before anyone saw the raincoated figure that had fallen from the bench to the pavement. The park patrolman noticed him finally, noticed the great swarm of pigeons that circled and squabbled. Falling, Mr. Norton had broken open the two large bags he carried: one of bread crumbs, one of peanuts. And the pigeons were fighting over him.

.   .   .

Aurelie sighed and dabbed at her eyes when they told her, and went off to arrange for the funeral. "Dear dear," she said, "I'm afraid that comes of giving up whisky." She also bought herself a black dress. "My very worst color. I look horribly sallow in black."

Joan refused to go to the funeral. "Do him up without me."

"I don't think I'll go either," Doris said. And there was a flash of something that could have been fear in her face.

"Honestly," Aurelie said, "you girls have such bad manners."

"I'm sure you can manage without us."

"Sure," Doris said. "You won't need us to beat off the banshees."

Joan said, "Did you decide where you're going to put him?"

That had been the other problem. Mr. Norton, who had been born in Bristol, Tennessee, did not have a burial plot.

"Put him in with Grandmama," Joan suggested.

Aurelie looked horrified. "That is my family tomb."

Doris chuckled. "Honey baby, he *is* your family."

But finally they found a separate little plot for Mr. Norton. Way in back of the cemetery, bordering along the L&N tracks.

Several days later Aurelie, Doris, and Joan went up to the attic apartment and gathered up clothes and

216 / THE HOUSE ON COLISEUM STREET

linens and cleared out the closets, which were packed
with empty whisky bottles. Drew the curtains and covered the furniture with old sheets. Books and charts and
instruments and dress swords and uniforms went into
trunks whose lids were slammed down and locked. Finally.

"Well," Aurelie said at the end of the day, "a sad,
sad job."

Doris's face gleamed with sweat. "If I'd had to carry
one more basket of empty bottles down those stairs I'd
have dropped in my tracks."

"It's finished," Aurelie said.

"It's really empty now," Joan said.

The traces of Herbert Norton were gone. There were
just two large rooms, dusky with their shutters drawn,
humped with sheeted furniture. They had been emptied. Finally and completely.

When Aurelie and her daughters left, they locked the
door behind them. The spiders and the mice could take
over.

JOAN thought: the hurt will stop when I'm pregnant. When all that empty space is filled up.

For one flash second she thought: it's a pity you have to have a man for it. It would be so much nicer if it just happened. If each time the little ovum burst out it carried a full child, instead of just half a one. If you could just say this is my child, and not just half mine. . . .

She laughed at herself and stopped thinking that.

I want to be great and round, she thought. And rest my hands on my belly. Folded hands resting and waiting. Feeling your body grow great and large and expand and fill the world. Filling the world with your seed.

Sending children out one after the other. Like meteors flying off a sun. Children one after the other. Following in the steps of that first ghost child. . . . Ghost child, lost child.

Would they always follow it, she thought. Would they always be following that little piece of seaweed, red seaweed.

She dreamt about it sometimes. Could see it so plain: big-eyed and red, drifting in its ocean.

And she always woke up, her insides churning with fright. She would have to put the light on and sit and stare at the bulb until the dry white light reassured her. Even so, after one of those dreams she felt vaguely frightened and upset all day long. She took a couple of Dexedrines to make herself feel better.

And in the evenings there was Fred. They had dinner each night now. Sometimes he picked her up. Sometimes she met him at his office.

Her father had had an office in that same building. Now and then, in the elevators, in the halls, she and Fred met people who would remember: "Anthony Mitchell's daughter. . . . My dear, he had pictures of you all over his office. Not just one on the desk. Not for Mitchell. All over the walls. Named his boat for you too, or was it a horse. . . ."

"I wish I hadn't been so young when he died," she told Fred.

He just nodded.

"You think that's silly?"

"Well," Fred said evenly, "it's better to remember things than really see them."

"No," she said, "it wouldn't have been that way."

She liked meeting Fred at his office, liked opening the frosted glass door that had his name on it, liked having the secretaries watch her, liked leaving with him, liked walking down the white corridors with him, the streaked marble corridors that looked cracked and dirty and smelled of pine oil.

Each day now. He skipped the handball he had always played on Wednesday. He said nothing, and she did not ask. But she was quietly grateful.

One evening she said simply: "I'm tired of cars. Makes it seem so awful somehow and sordid."

So after dinner, each evening, they went directly back to his apartment. She had never been there before alone. She had always been ashamed. Now she did not care. Not any longer. They walked boldly in the yard and she felt her backbone stiff and proud.

A couple of days later she stopped using her diaphragm.

Fred said, "I think we ought to celebrate whatever makes you so happy."

She considered telling him, then decided against it. "I don't know," she said, "I just feel good."

It seemed to her sometimes that they went rushing straight from dinner to bed. Sometimes the speed bothered her. And she would make up little excuses: "Let's go to the French Market and have some coffee."

But when they were there it was always she who was first ready to leave. Not Fred.

I'm like a bitch in heat, she thought. Shameless groveling bitch.

She nodded her head emphatically. Fred chuckled. She glanced up at him suddenly, her skin jumping with alarm. She had forgotten him.

She blinked rapidly and looked around, remembering back along the evening. Trying to set herself securely on this tiny spot of time that she was occupying. Trying for balance, delicately like a dancer.

They were in Galatoire's, having dinner. The small noisy room, the mirrored walls, the dragonfly forms of the overhead fans, the cash register clicking in back . . .

She took a deep breath and was secure again. She had come here since she was a child.

"Where were you?" Fred asked.

"I do kind of drift in and out, I guess."

"Anywhere I'd be interested in?"

"No," she said.

They did not mention marriage again. Sometimes it seemed to Joan that they were already married. Seemed that they had been together so close so constantly for a very long time.

And sometimes she was surprised to find how happy she was with him. Surprised because she knew he wasn't the right man at all.

JOAN told the passage of time by the marks of the short cold winter. She noticed the frosts and marked their brown lines on the banana trees, each wave cutting lower. Like a brown tide, but reversed. Each one cutting down the tree until there was only a bare staff jutting up. By summer they would be eight feet high again, with their drooping purple flowers and hanging clusters of bananas.

She noticed the crisp deep blue of the sky—a sky that was never seen except for the short months of winter. She floated under it, and as she did, she studied it carefully. The way she studied all the things about her. She studied its brilliant deep unbroken color. Like bright blue china. Like the inside of a teacup put over the earth.

A great big teacup. For days after that she felt positively friendly toward the sky. Familiar. The way you would feel toward a piece of china you had seen since you were a child. The whole world was very peaceful and very quiet.

And quite suddenly, it ended. Ended with the few seconds it took her to recognize the car.

THE street light showed it plainly. There was a convertible parked in front of the house on Coliseum Street. A yellow Ford convertible, several years old. It was washed and polished.

She had been in that car once. It was clean and washed when they began too. But the roads they had driven had left their dust on the hood and fenders, had left their sting in their eyes and their taste on lips. . . .

It was so simple. She felt herself go deathly cold. All of a sudden. Like the last seconds of an anesthetic.

She got out of Fred's car steadily, easily. She heard her heels clicking on the brick sidewalk as she walked to the gate. She heard herself saying, "Doris seems to have a date."

Fred took her to the heavy lead-glass door. "A big Saturday night."

"Won't you come in?"

"Now that," he laughed, "is a formal invitation. . . .

223

Maybe they don't want company. Ever think of that?"

The words might have hurt once. But not now. The anesthetic had taken effect. She wasn't there any more.

She put her purse and gloves on the hall table, under the lamp with the beaded fringe. She took off her coat and dropped it on the fragile Louis XIV chair that had been Aurelie's wedding present from her third husband.

She looked around for Fred, saw that he was not there. She wondered. . . . Thinking hard, she remembered kissing him good night at the door.

The door to the little living room, the one that Aurelie called the second parlor, was closed. There were voices behind it. Clinking glass and two voices. Joan recognized them.

She walked over and opened the door.

She did not quite know what she had expected. But she was surprised to see only a couple facing each other, shoeless feet propped on a coffee table between the two chairs.

"For God's sake," Doris said.

Michael wiggled his toes under their black socks. "Hi."

His hair was rumpled, standing straight up on top, its hair oil glistening. As if a hand had run through it. His very fair skin had taken on a deep flush and his dark beardline stood out stronger than ever against the pink.

If I got close to him, Joan found herself thinking, I'd find out that there'd be a batch of little red veins appearing around his nose. And spreading out across his cheeks. Like cobwebs.

The radio was playing very softly in one corner. Joan turned her eyes to it slowly. Masses of strings were slithering slowly up and down.

"It sounds like *Frère Jacques*," she said irrelevantly.

"Old duck," Doris said, "go away."

She's drunk, Joan thought, I've never seen her so drunk before.

And her eyes focused on the tray right beside Michael's feet. A little round tray, two bottles and a pitcher of water. And an ice bucket. A silver ice bucket. . . .

"That's mine," Joan said.

"It is not," Doris said. "You gave it to Aurelie."

She had, of course. Only last Christmas, with a burst of feeling, she had gone into a jewelers and asked to see the Danish silver. She had bought an ice bucket with ivory handles. When Aurelie said, "You shouldn't have," she answered simply, "But I felt like it." She had. Afterward though she wondered why. She didn't really like her mother very much.

"Go away, old duck," Doris repeated. And fluttered her hands, as if she was chasing chickens.

Michael waved at her, mockingly, a child's wave, stiff wrist and moving fingers.

"Out," Doris said, "out."

Joan turned then and left. Only it wasn't so much leaving as it was fleeing. She could feel panic shaking her body like a chill.

She got to the hall and sat down on top of her coat on the little Louis XIV chair. Somebody got up and slammed the door shut. Even through it she could hear them laughing.

She sat perfectly still. After a few minutes she tipped her head back and rested it against the wall. She did not move again.

She did not know exactly how long she sat there, not thinking, not listening really. Just waiting. And she did not know what she was waiting for.

She did not move when she heard the steps on the front porch, and she scarcely turned her head when Aurelie opened the door and stepped into the hall, her deep laugh swirling around her like a flip of a scarf, carelessly.

Somebody was with her, somebody stood just outside the door.

Joan watched the shock on Aurelie's face turn to annoyance. I ruined an entrance for her, she thought dully.

"Child, child," Aurelie said, "whatever are you doing?"

"Something wrong?" a man stepped through the door.

Even in the little half-light of the hall Joan could see him clearly. Short, stocky, balding, with the remains of blond hair cut close to his head.

"You're ruining your coat," Aurelie said.

Joan stood up, shook the coat and hung it across her

arm. She nodded toward the closed door of the little parlor.

Aurelie marched over to it, with her most determined step. The man followed her, more softly. He gave Joan a quick glance as he passed.

"I'm Joan," she said quietly, automatically. "The oldest."

She had been identifying herself to Aurelie's friends that way for years.

She looked at the man more curiously as he passed close by her. He was very blond; his skin was sunburned a deep tan and there were millions of little crisscrossing lines in it.

He looks all right, Joan found herself thinking. I bet anything she marries him. . . .

Aurelie pulled open the door. "For heaven's sake!"

They weren't sitting apart any longer. They were together in one armchair. Joan turned away.

"For heaven's sake," Aurelie said again. "I seem to have come home just in time!"

Joan went over and sat down on the lowest of the steps leading upstairs. She patted the carpet with one hand, slowly. That's what she's going to be, she thought, the highly outraged mama.

Aurelie had been saying something else. Joan listened. "Leave this house right now." A pause. "Shall I ask Mr. Bryan to help you out?"

Mr. Bryan pulled himself up, taking a deep breath, like a fighter.

Joan thought: strutting like a rooster. And Bryan is an Irish name. He looks like the sort of man who would have sons. And isn't it a shame Aurelie can't have any more children. . . .

Aurelie was saying: "I'm just shocked. Just absolutely shocked."

Joan saw Mr. Bryan move over closer to Aurelie, protectively, so that his shoulder was almost touching hers.

"Oh God," Joan said softly under her breath.

Michael got his coat on and walked to the door, with the exaggerated steadiness of the very drunk. "It has been a most pleasant evening, Miss Doris," he mocked formally.

Doris followed him. Aurelie stood perfectly still in the parlor door. Mr. Bryan stood beside her like a watchful poodle. Joan looked down at the outline of her knees through the thin silk of her dress.

At the door Doris caught Michael's arm and whispered something to him. He gave a quick heel-clicking bow.

Doris turned and leaned against the closed door. "Boy oh boy," she said, very quietly. "Remind me to stick needles into you sometime."

Joan did not look up.

Doris walked by her and up the stairs. As she passed Joan caught a whiff of perfume. *Mitsouko*. It was her scent. The bottle was on her dresser; she could see the round flat shape. Or maybe it wasn't any more.

She turned and said to the climbing legs above her: "Did you take the bottle or did you just use it?"

Without stopping Doris turned her head, symbolically spitting to one side.

Joan felt very tired. She put her head down on her knees and began to listen to her breathing.

"Child, child," Aurelie said, "you must be exhausted. Go on up to bed."

"Are you all right?" Mr. Bryan said.

Joan got to her feet very slowly. She brushed down her skirt, picked up her coat and gloves and purse. "We've always had very bad luck with the men in this house," she said calmly. "You have just seen the last example."

Mr. Bryan looked startled. His eyes, which were a light brown, like the shell of a pecan, blinked once.

Aurelie laughed. A true chuckle. Mr. Bryan's eyes lighted up again. "I hope you don't have many like that," he said.

"We all have bad luck," Joan said, and went upstairs. "Even I have bad luck. And I don't get many to have it with."

"You see," Aurelie said to her departing back, "my daughters are all individualists."

"Yes," Mr. Bryan said. But he sounded doubtful. The pecan-colored eyes might be just a bit darker.

"Would you like a nightcap?" Aurelie asked.

Joan went into her room and closed the door.

.   .   .

She had been lying in bed quite awhile, lying across the bed, muscles rigid.

She heard Mr. Bryan leave. Heard him whistle his way across the sidewalk and start up his car with a cheery roar. She heard him spin around the corner with a screech of rubber.

I think, she told herself quietly, I'll call him Papa. And I wonder what he would say if I did.

She heard Aurelie come up to bed. Heard the old pipes rattle with quick running water. Then the thick early morning silence. At a quarter past the hour a street-car rattled past over on the avenue, rattled off into the distance with a hollow metallic jangle. There would be nothing more for an hour. An occasional car went by too, a light brushing sound of tires. But it was all very far away from the house on Coliseum Street.

She got up and opened her windows, letting the clear cold air slip into the musty room.

The house had a definite smell, she thought. And all the cleaning in the world would never get it out. Because it wasn't a smell of dirt. It wasn't a smell of cooking. Or of anything in particular. It was the smell of everything. Of everything that had gone on in the house for the past hundred and twenty years. It was the smell of the people and the things. Of the living that had gone on between the walls.

The smell of the generations being born. Dying. And being laid out in the front parlor with a sprig of sweet olive from the door in their clenched hand.

People left their smells behind them. It was almost like the paper you'd cut dolls out of—the dolls were gone but you could see their shape and size and form. You could see just the way they had been.

It seemed to her sometimes that she could hear them too. That they left little sounds behind them, echoing around the walls. Like faint rustly mice. Seemed she could hear the sounds of all their breathing. Left-behind breathing. Echoing. Gently, like leaves.

Still dressed, she reached down and pulled the quilt over her.

She lay and listened to the rustling of time past. Her musty grandfathers, echoing from the St. Louis Cemetery. And heard the rustling of the future time. And tried to understand it. And gave up finally, sadly.

I wanted none of the things that have happened, she thought. None of the things that have happened. They just came along. I didn't intend them. Time and things like a river, passing.

Before me, she thought, and after me. Things will go on happening when I am dead. Pass around me and over me and go on.

And instead of being frightened, she felt comforted.

She had lain there she didn't know how long when she heard the footsteps. She heard them first on the cement of the sidewalk, then on the brick of the path. And in between she heard the slight rusty squeak of the front gate.

She slipped out of bed, moving gently inside her

clothes so that they didn't rustle and spoil her hearing. She got to the window and looked down. She saw nothing. She was too high and the space between the houses was too narrow. She would have had to lift the screen and look straight down into the deep dark of the pathway.

She crouched by the open window and felt the cold night air pour over her. Like a river.

Nonsensically she found herself singing, silently: we shall gather at the river, the beautiful, beautiful river. . . . That was all she knew. That was all she had learned. Aurelie didn't approve of her girls learning and singing Protestant hymns.

The sound of uncertain steps on old slippery mossy brick: hollow sound of bricks set in cinder. Then a quick flurry, a rush, a grunt.

Her ears pinpointed the noise in the night. She couldn't see but she didn't have to. Somebody had leaped for the lowest rung of the fire escape, the iron fire escape that led to the empty attic rooms where Herbert Norton had once lived. And somebody caught hold of the iron bars, caught hold with a little hissing grunt and swung up.

The ladder was a dozen feet from her window. Holding her breath, she leaned against the screen and stared at the figure that emerged from the dark, climbing quickly, outlined against the bricks.

She caught a scent, clear in the still air. And she recognized it: Aphrodisia. He has good taste, she thought. He had not worn it the day they went across the lake.

But then, she thought, he hadn't been dressed up then. It hadn't been anything special.

The fire escape passed close by the bathroom window, which Aurelie had always kept nervously locked. It was open now.

Joan listened. And followed the little sounds through the bathroom, into the hall and back again into Doris's room. Once she heard a muffled giggle.

The wind ruffled the hair at the nape of her neck. It was very cold and she shivered. She held her hands straight out in front of her and studied the nails. But in the dark she could see nothing.

All of a sudden she knew what she had been waiting for. She knew what she was going to do.

Joan opened her own door, moved out in the hall. She hesitated, noticing for the first time in the still night air how the sharp sweet odor of rats hung about the house.

Then she was moving down the hall, silently, with only the light rustle of her silk dress. (I'm still dressed, she thought. I forgot. The same dress I was wearing for dinner with Fred. And that was such a long time ago. A very, very long time ago. And Fred, now, I will miss him.)

She closed the front door behind her, and moved off down the street.

Michael's voice was echoing in her head: "If it had come out, honey bunch, I'd be fired so fast I wouldn't even see the door slamming."

She found herself running, on tiptoe, silently, quickly.

SHE knew the house she wanted—a square box of yellowing stucco, set on a foot-high terrace. In the dark (the entrance light was turned off) she stumbled on the steps. She climbed them wearily, and it seemed that she would never get to the top, though there were only seven of them. She felt around the door until she found the bell.

She rang, timidly at first, then with more and more insistence. A light came on upstairs. A window opened and someone called: "Who is it?"

She did not answer. She stood under a little portico, hidden from sight. She kept ringing. While she waited, she fingered the scraggly tendrils of the Confederate jasmine that twisted around the entrance.

A hall light. A clatter as the door unlocked.

A not very friendly mutter: "What is this about?"

"Dean Lattimore?"

A grunted yes.

"Would you mind asking me in?" Joan said. "It's

quite cold out here and I seem to have forgotten my coat."

Afterward, looking back, and trying very hard, she found she could not remember parts of that morning. She could not remember going into the house. But she did remember being in a room, a living room that was half dark. There were only two lamps on. And the room itself was not very tidy. There were newspapers on the floor in a little heap, and butts in the ash trays. A couple of glasses still stood on the table, one with the froth marks of beer.

It was all so familiar. As if she'd been here before, saying the same things. As if it had all been done so long ago.

She remembered being very quiet, very assured. She remembered smoothing out her skirt carefully before she sat down. She remembered crossing her ankles, properly.

And she stepped out of herself. She stepped back, far back, and watched. It was like watching a movie screen. She was not involved at all. Sometimes she didn't even hear the words. Sometimes she could see her own lips moving and she knew that she was talking but she did not seem to hear the words. And then the sound would come back. . . .

"A horrible time, I know. But if I didn't come now I wouldn't have come. Because I have to steel myself up for this. . . ."

As she went along she knew that she was not telling the truth, not the whole truth. That she was changing it slightly, very slightly. That she was deliberately destroying a man.

She knew it and it did not matter to her. She had no control any more. She did not feel vicious. She was not afraid. She did not feel anything at all. Except not part of herself any more.

"He drove me across the lake. We were just going for a spin across the causeway, but we didn't stop once we got on the other side. . . . He brought beer out to the car and we drank can after can. . . . He told his class he was sick. . . ."

Michael was so very handsome. White skin, dark eyes. Delicate face for a man.

"I didn't believe it at first. . . ."

There was a cigar butt in the room somewhere. They really should have thrown it out. Dead cigars smelled terrible. Aurelie would never have left a cigar butt in her living room. . . .

She saw herself lean back in her chair and rub her fingers against her temples. There was a question. She shook her head. "I'm sorry," she said, "I didn't hear you."

"And who arranged this—this thing for you?"

She shrugged and lied deliberately. "He did. It was his."

She used to believe that the earth would open and swallow you if you told a lie. . . .

There was a woman in the room, Joan noticed. A grey-haired woman in a dark red dressing gown. Deans were always married, of course.

"He told me not to say anything, that it would ruin his career."

The dean snorted. "If this is true, young lady, it certainly has."

Joan stared at the windows. They had shades instead of Venetian blinds, and one of the shades was pulled slightly crooked.

"One other thing," she found herself saying, "you might wonder why I came now. . . ." They always liked to know the why of things. They always liked to have reasons. Neat and nice. She could give them a reason; it wouldn't be true but it would be neat. "He's started on my sister, my little sister. . . ." She heard a sharp breath from the dean's wife. It does sound good, she thought. "Only tonight my mother had to ask him to leave the house. . . ."

Aurelie, Aurelie, you'll have to say that it's true, because you won't dare not to.

It's still pitch black outside, because I can see our reflections as sharp as in a mirror.

"If this is true . . ."

"You can check." Of course they could. There was just enough truth about it. They would find that out at once. And they would think that the rest was true too.

She could hear Michael's words echoing around in her head: "I'd be fired so fast. . . ."

Michael, Michael where are you right now? You don't know what's happened. And when you do it will be all over. . . . By then I won't be in love with you any more. I'm almost not now.

"I'm going to leave, of course. I'll have to leave."

And where would she go? There had to be somewhere. It didn't seem to matter. Not that much. She could always go somewhere.

She put her hands on her knees and pushed herself upright. "Thank you for your time."

She was finished. She had done what she had to do. Now she could start to forget. The stand of pine and the soft needles. The early morning trip on the coast, with the bugs splattering on the windshield.

It was ended now, the whole thing.

"You're not going to walk out at this hour?"

"I walked here."

"Now really."

"I have to walk. It's the only way I can go."

"Where is your coat?"

"I left it at home. I forgot to take anything."

"You simply must have a sweater. I'll get one in a second."

When she left it was with a sweater around her shoulders. A sweater that smelt foreign and strange and musty with old bureau drawers and perfume that had gone stale and harsh.

When she stepped into the clear cold air she realized that that house too had the sweet sick odor of rats in it.

Does it get more intense at night or do we just not notice it during the day?

She walked on steadily. . . . Look once more, then start to forget. . . . Down the paths, among the trees, the trees that had no smell this cold night, the hot-weather trees. . . . Past the library, dark and closed; and who was that couple? The one I saw, only I didn't really, way upstairs where no one ever went, only I did. . . . Along the brick walks, through the lines of azaleas, shoulder high, spotted with an occasional early flower. They liked the cold; they would flame out in a month or so. And where did the couples go, the mating couples that huddled behind these azaleas on the hot nights of spring and summer and fall? And where did they go?

I used to park my car over there, and I would walk this way. Before. A long time before. And I would see the little light on the gas dial glow up the inside of the car and I would close the door and be secure and safe inside my steel shell.

She passed a watchman's station. He was sitting in the tiny room, warming something on a little electric plate. He heard her heels and he came to the door and stood to watch her pass. "Good evening," she said, graciously. He touched his cap, halfway. And he looked after her until she went around the line of bushes and was out of sight.

She passed through the gates, the imitation Spanish gates that had the plaque of the class of 1905.

I came this way that morning and I saw him in the window and he came down and we went hunting for owls.

Her heels clattered on the iron bridge over the deepest gutter. And it's here that there was ice once. Years ago. Real ice that lasted a long time into the day, even after the sun came up. And that's where the hibiscus bush is, the yellow one I used to pick every day last summer, every single day on the way to class. Only it's frozen down now so there're only some hollow brown stalks standing up; it will have to grow back right from the roots when it gets warm again.

The pavement was uneven now; tree roots had thrown it up. She went more slowly, being careful of her footing.

And then she stood in front of the house on Coliseum Street. I'll own it some day, she thought, because I'm the oldest and Aurelie will leave it to the oldest, whether she likes me or not. A tall narrow house, with an iron fence in front and a balcony across the second floor. There were no lights showing, only a glow deep inside.

Maybe I can come back to it. And maybe I won't even want to. Maybe. But I'll have to go away now.

She stood directly in front of the gate and looked up at the house.

I'm standing right where that tramp stood. Right where he stood that day. Last summer. The day Michael called for the first time. . . . And he stood out here and he must have been sick because he couldn't seem to stay on his feet. And the police came for him. . . .

She looked down the uneven pavement, smeared with grease by the falling camphor berries, rising in little chunks with the pressure of the tree roots underneath. He had stood and swayed and fallen and lain there, muttering something. And there wasn't anything left of it. . . . There wasn't anything left of the child either, that had lived in the world and walked about and nobody had seen it and nobody knew it was there, listening. Ghost child.

She had disturbed a mockingbird. Directly overhead he shifted and fluttered and sent down a half line of song, sleepily.

I could stand anything, she thought, if it wasn't so lonely. If I could get pregnant again, I wouldn't be so lonely. At least not for that time. There'd be two everywhere I went then, for a while.

In the center of the tiny yard the tile fountain gurgled gently. The bronze dolphins leered and squirted obscenely. It was the one mark her father had made on the house on Coliseum Street. Joan thought: Except for me.

And I'll have to go away now. Once they know what I've done, I couldn't stay in the house. But I can go. It's only a question of where. My father knew I would have to leave some day. And he fixed it so I can go. . . .

And she bowed slightly to the crisp busy figure on the other side of the grave.

She opened the gate—the iron was icy cold under her hand—and went up to the door, the heavy door with its thick pane of cut crystal. The brass knob was colder than the iron. She turned and nothing happened. It was locked. Of course. It would have locked after her.

She did not have a key. She had not thought to bring one with her. She stared for a bit at the knob that turned uselessly in her hand. Then she took one of the porch chairs and sat down in it and waited. It was quite cold in the early morning, and occasionally she shivered. Once she moved her chair to the spot the sun would strike first. Then she curled up, huddled inside her borrowed sweater, and waited. The water of the tile fountain turned lead-colored in the first light. The sun was beginning to come up.

$\mathcal{V}$oices of the $\mathcal{S}$outh

Doris Betts, *The Astronomer and Other Stories*

Sheila Bosworth, *Almost Innocent*

Erskine Caldwell, *Poor Fool*

Fred Chappell, *The Gaudy Place*

Fred Chappell, *It Is Time, Lord*

Ellen Douglas, *A Lifetime Burning*

Ellen Douglas, *The Rock Cried Out*

George Garrett, *An Evening Performance*

George Garrett, *Do, Lord, Remember Me*

Shirley Ann Grau, *The House on Coliseum Street*

Shirley Ann Grau, *The Keepers of the House*

Barry Hannah, *The Tennis Handsome*

William Humphrey, *Home from the Hill*

Mac Hyman, *No Time For Sergeants*

Madison Jones, *A Cry of Absence*

Willie Morris, *The Last of the Southern Girls*

Louis D. Rubin, Jr., *The Golden Weather*

Evelyn Scott, *The Wave*

Lee Smith, *The Last Day the Dogbushes Bloomed*

Elizabeth Spencer, *The Salt Line*

Elizabeth Spencer, *The Voice at the Back Door*

Allen Tate, *The Fathers*

Peter Taylor, *The Widows of Thornton*

Robert Penn Warren, *Band of Angels*

Robert Penn Warren, *Brother to Dragons*

Joan Williams, *The Morning and the Evening*